(Welcome To Hell, Book #4)

By
Eve Langlais

Copyright and Disclaimer

Prologue

"What is she?" The speaker didn't inquire with the repugnance Jenny had grown accustomed to but more with a sincere curiosity.

A finger poked at Jenny, stroking wet bangs from her face, exposing her features. She bore it in silence, not just because she feared a cuff for speaking out of turn but also out of awe, stunned by the beauty surrounding her. Women with the longest, most beautiful golden tresses circled her. How she envied them their silky yellow hair, especially when compared to her own greenish-hued strands, which kinked and curled wildly when dry.

"Is it a girl or a fish?"

A common question given Jenny's upper body was ivory white and smooth while her lower body shimmered with iridescent scales. However, she had legs, not a fishtail, to her mother's eternal shame. How many times had she heard, "Proper mermaids have a tail, fins, and gills."? All Jenny possessed were webbed toes and an ability to hold her breath for almost fifteen minutes. Needless to say, she didn't spend much time in the water with the other children her age. Heck, according to the midwives, she'd almost drowned at birth before they realized her affliction.

"Can she understand us do you think?" Pretty blue eyes framed in delicate lashes peered at her. "Can you speak, child?"

Jenny nodded but kept her lips clamped.

"What's your name? Where did you come from?"

She pointed to the water lapping at the rocky beach, a sandy, wet beach she'd awoken on, alone.

"Are you from across the Styx? Did your ship wreck on the shore?"

A frown wrinkled her nose. The Styx? What was that? Her home was under the waves of the Darkling Sea. Jenny shook her head.

The pretty ladies, with legs, not tails, wearing gauzy dresses of filmy material trimmed in feathers and bright flowers, clustered, tossing the occasional puzzled glance her way. Jenny huddled tighter.

If they were attempting subtlety, they failed. She could hear their dulcet muttering. Defective mermaid gene didn't mean she was deaf.

"Where do you think she came from? How did she get here?" the shortest one whispered.

"Does it really matter? She's here now and without a soul to vouch for her. If she did wreck here, then whoever she traveled with either drowned or got eaten by a monster from the Styx or sea."

"What should we do?" asked the plump one.

"What do you mean?"

"I mean, should we keep her? Considering she didn't drown, then she's obviously a gift."

"How do you figure that? She could just be a good swimmer."

"Or someone intentionally dumped her here," said the tallest one.

A single pair of suspicious eyes turned to Jenny, appraising and judging. "Maybe she's a trap?"

Three other pairs of eyes glanced her way as the rest of them now also weighed in. Jenny hugged her knees and dropped her gaze to her bare toes.

The plump one giggled. "Oh, really, Thelxiope. You and your conspiracy theories. A trap? Really? She's but a child. Not a bomb."

"I don't like it. She's obviously not one of us." Thelxiope didn't even bother to hide her distrust.

"She's not like anything," mused the tall one. "Or at least nothing I've encountered in my travels or books."

"I say we toss her back to the Styx or into the sea. Let the monsters deal with her."

Jenny cringed. She might not know where she was, but she couldn't help but think it would beat a swim with ferocious creatures.

Plump arms wrapped around her protectively. "Thelxiope! What is wrong with you? She's just a child!"

A child abandoned. A child not wanted. A child who didn't know what she was or where to go. *I fit in nowhere.*

A disdainful snort came from the distrustful one. "Do what you will. But don't say I didn't warn you."

"We are not tossing her out like rubbish," the tall one declared as she crouched before Jenny, placing herself eye to eye. In a gentle voice she asked, "What do you want us to do, little one?"

They were giving her a choice? Since when did Jenny have a say?

"I know you can understand us," the short, lovely lady with the smooth voice said. "I can see it in your face. Answer my sister, Raidne. The truth now. Tell us, what do you want us to do? Are you lost? Do you need us to find your parents?"

A vehement shake of Jenny's head answered that question. As far as she knew, her mother was the one who dumped her. Somehow she didn't think her less-than-loving parent would welcome Jenny's return.

"Do you have anywhere to go?" asked Raidne.

A sad shake.

"Would you like to stay here, with us?"

Truly? Peeking around at all the gorgeous faces, not sensing any real danger, even from the one with the suspicious eyes, Jenny wondered if they meant it. The warm breeze on her skin felt so nice, especially for one used to the coldness of waves and the damp cool of the caves. The scent of something sweet tickled her nose, tempting her to find out what emitted such a lovely smell. It was so different here. So … nice.

Jenny mustered up the courage to speak softly. "Do you truly mean it? Can I stay?"

Once the rain of insects and circling gulls tapered, the ground littered with twitching bodies, and the screaming stopped—by a sailor who'd happened to row to the island while the pretty ladies conversed—it was decided Jenny could remain, but only if she agreed on some singing lessons. And to speak as little as possible while she learned some control, lest she completely destroy all the island life. Lucky for her, the sirens proved immune to her strange vocal skill.

Thus did the orphan—with the killer voice—who wasn't quite sure what she was became an honorary siren and adopted niece to the four who lived there. While Jenny never quite managed to lure sailors to their shores to do her bidding—usually her singing sent them rowing the other way—she did manage to make many of them deaf, drive several insane, and even more beg for an end to their misery.

But at least she had a home.

Chapter One

On the docks by the River Styx…

"You've been a bad kitty." Lucifer shook his head at the hellcat in question, wearing a pained expression that his daughter, Muriel, would probably recognize. That chit knew how to push his buttons too.

Felipe, the minion in trouble, sat on his furry haunches alongside his catch—a thirty-foot-long sea serpent currently being measured by the local butcher. He hung his giant feline head, whiskers drooping.

"Don't try that innocent look with me. It might soften that witch who took you in, but it won't work with me, you rascal." Wearing his sternest expression—practiced often in front of a mirror to ensure he achieved the right effect—Lucifer berated the incorrigible cat. Not that it had any effect. Again, just like his mischievous daughter, the hell kitty thrived on driving him crazy. But at the same time, how could he stay mad at the minion who, in his youthful exuberance, sinned?

Still though, there was breaking the rules, and there was disrespect. One would get rewards—and kitty treats from Lucifer. The other needed curbing.

Shifting shapes until he stood as a man, with his hands covering his man parts, Felipe wore a sheepish expression on his face. "Would it help to say I was sorry?"

"No, but I appreciate your attempt to lie." Lucifer paced in agitation on the quay and stabbed his finger at the cat. "What have I told you about playing with the Styx monsters?"

"Don't."

"And what did you do? Don't answer that. I'd say that part was obvious. So what do you have to say for yourself?" Crossing his arms over his chest, Lucifer fixed him with a stern glare.

Felipe rolled his shoulders in a shrug. "I was hungry."

"Then you go to the market."

"But it's not as fresh." The handsome hellcat pouted, and Lucifer fought not to smile.

The shape-shifter truly had the gift of charm, and he knew it. It was why he did so well with the women, the lucky bastard. *Unlike some of us stuck in a monogamous relationship.* Blech. Even thinking the word made Lucifer feel ill. The things he did for great sex—and Mother Nature's apple pie, the baked kind, not the one between her legs. That one was pure honey.

His old friend Charon, who stood alongside watching the exchange from the dark depths of his cowl, threw up his gloved hands. "Hungry? Too fucking bad. That's the second one you've killed this month. How am I supposed to properly awe the newly damned I'm shipping across the river if we don't have any impressive specimens to scare the pants off them?"

"I think you should worry more about your son and his reputation of screwing up than my fishing habits," Felipe retorted. "Or did you not tell our lord about his latest mishap?"

Not another one. Lucifer fought to not bang his head off a hard object. "What did Adexios do this time?" Lucifer demanded. "Did he overturn the boat again? Lose his oar?"

"I'd rather not say," Charon mumbled.

A smirk on his lips, Felipe didn't have a problem tattling. "He let one of the newly damned pilot his boat while he took a nap. The damned one immediately turned the boat around and poled it back to land."

Counting to ten didn't make the news any easier to bear, but Lucifer reined in his temper instead of blasting the bearer of the tidings into meaty chunks. He had better uses for the cat. "Are you trying to tell me I've got some newbies running around on the mortal plane instead of down in processing?"

Given the number of souls arriving daily, Lucifer had only enough time to meet the special or most intriguing cases. However, no one could think to accuse him of slacking on the job, even if he didn't meet or greet each damned one by name, because he ran a tight administration. Every soul that arrived got its just desserts. No bad deed went unpunished, or unapplauded.

"The good news is they're still more or less in the pit." Felipe wore a gloating grin, and Lucifer just knew he wouldn't like the rest of his news.

"I hear a big but coming."

"They're just not within the nine circles. While Adexios snoozed, the temporary boatman dumped him and then managed to steer the boat with its passengers to Siren Isle. So the damned ones are contained. The bad news is it won't be easy getting them back." Felipe snickered as Charon groaned.

"Bloody Hell. You know how I hate dealing with those women." Not to mention Mother Nature had banned him from visiting their isles. Apparently she didn't trust him around gals who could sing a man into doing anything they wanted. As if that sexy bunch needed to enchant him to get him to drop his pants. All he needed was a come-hither look, and he was ready to go. Or he used to be until he got a girlfriend who insisted on monogamy. Ah for the good old days when the witches used to dance around bonfires, naked, and invite him over to the mortal realm for orgies.

Folding his robed arms over his chest, his hands hidden in the voluminous sleeves, the full-time boatman of the Styx sighed. "I'll send my lad to get them back."

"And have him fuck something else up?" Lucifer snapped. "No, thank you. I think it's time I reassigned the boy to something a little less strenuous, and a lot less enjoyable. As for you—" Lucifer turned his mighty glare on the hellcat, who seemed entirely too pleased with himself. Time to rip the canary eating grin from his face. "Since you also disobeyed, don't think you're getting off scot-free. I've got a job for you. Get those souls back."

"But they're on Siren Isle."

"And?"

"Those females ensnare males and keep them as slaves."

"Then you'd better be careful."

"But—"

Drawing himself up, and letting the fires of Hell glow in his eyes— a neat trick he'd learned eons ago—Lucifer spoke. "NOW!" He might have yelled it. It sure did echo impressively, and it had the required effect. Felipe held his cocky tongue and nodded.

Inside, Lucifer chuckled with glee. As usual, things were going along as planned. His plan. His hellcat minion was about to meet the mother of his future litters. Or get enslaved by a bunch of sirens and turned into a stud.

Either way, his will would be done. And the ranks of his demonic legion would swell. For what purpose, he didn't yet know, but he had a sneaky feeling he'd have need of an army, and soon.

With a pout on his lips, Felipe shifted into his feline and bounded away to ready for his trip.

Charon shook his covered head. "He's trouble that one."

Perhaps, but a trouble Lucifer could understand and even admire. Fighting, wenching, and building a reputation. How he missed the old days, a time when he didn't have so many responsibilities and souls to care for—and torture. "Not as much trouble as your boy. What are we going to do with him? He's obviously not cut out for the job of ferryman."

"He just needs more time."

"Time?" Lucifer snorted and smoke curled from his nostrils. "The boy's a bloody idiot who couldn't find his way out of a room with an open door. There's got to be something he's good at other than creating paperwork for me. Doesn't everyone know my time is too valuable to waste on such trivial matters?" He could be shining his newest golf trophy, practicing his surfing for the upcoming king of the waves competition, or getting his knob polished by one talented earthshaker.

"Numbers."

"Say what?" Lucifer shook his head of the stray thoughts cluttering it.

A pained sigh escaped Charon. "I said Adexios is good with numbers. A useless skill, I know."

Lucifer rubbed his chin. "Numbers, eh? Actually, that might come in handy. I've been meaning to do a census." If trouble truly did approach, then he needed to know exactly where he stood.

"A census? I thought that's what the Hellacious Bureau of Statistics already did. I just about lost my mind filling in their latest one-hundred-page survey."

A chuckle rumbled in Lucifer's chest. "The minions running that department do enjoy their jobs a tad much. Damned bureaucrats. But, no, the census I'm speaking of has to do with the demons not on my radar, those born off the books and in the wilds."

"Wilds? You can't send my boy out there. He'd get eaten in a day!"

"Indeed he would." And if the boy belonged to any other minion, Lucifer wouldn't give it a second thought. However, he considered Charon a friend. "Still, the boy needs to earn his keep. Let me think about it more, and I'll get back to you."

"You're not going to kill him, are you? Not because I care," Charon hastened to mention. "But his mother would make my life an even worse Hell than the wondrous one you've created."

"Never fear, old friend. Death is too kind. Character building, though, in the form of adventure, danger, and mayhem, that's another thing." Not to mention Adexios was yet another person Lucifer could torture in his version of the matchmaking game. However, first, he had a hellcat in need of a leash and a collar, and he knew just the woman to snare him—and help him as an added bonus.

Chapter Two

"Fetch the missing souls, he says, as if I were a bloody hellhound instead of a rare and mighty hellcat," Felipe grumbled as he stuffed some clothes in a duffel bag.

Did Lucifer not understand what a waste of his talents retrieving those damned souls was? Felipe was a master hunter. He could track anything—and take it down. Just look at his impressive file, the monsters he'd conquered, the records he'd broken.

Any deaf minion could go to the sirens far away island and round up some escapees. Didn't Lucifer understand this task would cut into Felipe's more important tasks? Such as keeping the catacombs free of the giant two-headed rats so the miners could work without fear of getting eaten. Or tracking the delinquent damned souls who thought to skip out on their punishment. And what about beating the wenching record set by the demon Remy before he settled down with Ysabel, the witch?

"I swear, if I find out this stupid quest was arranged somehow by that no good fire demon, mated to Ysabel or not, I'll rip his dick off and feed it to the hounds."

No matter how he complained, though, Felipe doubted Remy was behind Lucifer's task. Having raised him since he was a wee cub, Ysabel would kill Remy if he so much as plucked a whisker from Felipe's chin, which irritated her demonic mate to no end.

"Stupid no good—"

"I hope you weren't talking about anyone we know," purred Lucifer in a deceivingly soft tone.

Felipe strangled an unmanly scream at the Lord of Hell's unexpected entrance. "My lord, I didn't hear you knock."

"As if I'd do anything so ordinary and mannerly."

"Was there something you forgot?" Or wanted to rescind? Say like one stupid job?

"Sometimes I forget we live in a more evolved age with hellphones and what not. It occurred to me after our conversation and my orders that I could call over to the sirens and demand they return my missing souls."

Demand? Only Lucifer would have the balls of steel required to demand anything from those independent women. There was a reason the sirens lived on an isle by the edge of the dark sea, alone and ungoverned. "Did they agree?"

Flopping onto his buttery smooth, demon-leather couch—with hand-stitched cushions—Lucifer's brows drew together in a straight line. "Not exactly. Thelxiope, the oldest of the sirens and the head bitch in charge, says she would have loved to have handed them back. Damned souls do them no good you know. They prefer live demons or mortals because only they have viable seed. Anyhow, apparently, my lost souls had the misfortune to meet Jenny as she was practicing her siren song and well…" Lucifer trailed off.

The failing of every feline raised its whiskered head. Curiosity prompted Felipe to ask, "What happened?" How bad could it be? The souls were already dead and couldn't die again unless they threw themselves in the abyss for the ultimate soul recycling. Hard to eternally punish the damned if they died too quick.

No one was quite sure how it worked, whether Lucifer himself controlled it or it was just the way it was, but any human who expired on the mortal plane and became a damned one couldn't quite die down in the pit. Feel pain, get injured, suffer torture, yes, but only the abyss could promise oblivion.

A grimace twisted the Dark Lord's lips. "Doesn't matter. Let's just say, they've been adequately punished and there's no longer a pressing need to fetch them, which means you're off the hook when it comes to collecting them."

"Yes!" Felipe fist pumped the air, unable to contain his joy. He acted too soon.

Lucifer wasn't done. "Which is good because I need you for another job."

No! Felipe kept that comment to himself. It never paid to antagonize the King of the Pit. Just ask the guy in the clock tower forced for eternity to call out the hour while flogging himself with a cat o' nine tipped in barbs. His punishment for arriving late to a meeting with Lucifer.

"For your new task, I'd like you to meet with and escort my newest recruit back to the inner ring for assignment."

Why did that sound deceivingly simple? "Who is the recruit, and where am I getting them from?"

"Jenny is on Siren Isle, and she needs a ride back here. Given her unique talents, I've decided she should join my awesome legion and become one of my special evil minions."

"Why can't she come herself?"

"It's complicated. Suffice it to say, I need you to accompany her. I'll have someone from Charon's fleet pole you over."

"If you've got a boat already going, then what do you need me for?"

"Firstly, to convince the chit to leave."

"I thought she was joining the legion."

"She is. She just doesn't know it yet."

"Have you asked her?"

"Of course not. Asking isn't something I do." Lucifer snorted. "Although, I did mention it to her guardians."

"And?"

"And the harpy in charge laughed as she declined. Did you know Thelxiope even had the nerve to use the words, no thank you?" Lucifer shuddered. "I'll bet they've trained the chit to have manners too. We'll have to break her of that bad habit. I will not tolerate politeness."

Again, common sense got overruled by instinct. "Why don't they want her to come to the capital? Doesn't this broad know the honor such a post brings?" Ass kissing. Never hang with Lucifer unless you planned to lay it on thick.

"Who knows why. She's a woman."

"Can't you just order her?"

Lucifer grimaced. "It pains me to admit, but Siren's Isle is kind of out of my jurisdiction. I lost it in a game of strip poker eons ago. I still say those wenches cheated. But they won, even if by underhanded means that involved a lot of naked titty. They've yet to accept a rematch. So, given the situation, I can't make them send Jenny to me."

"So teleport in, grab the girl, and teleport out before they even have a chance to notice."

Steam curled from Lucifer's nose. "Are you doing on purpose to point out my difficulties with that damned isle? Portals don't work in and around the isle. Something to do with the interdimensional rift they've got to the mortal world to snare their sailors."

"Sorry, boss. I wasn't aware of that. That's a bitch."

"Pain in my ass more like, but since I rarely have a need for anything from them, not usually an issue. Except for now. I want Jenny."

"Aren't you afraid Mother Nature will have a jealous fit?" When the Queen of Green threw a fit, the whole world knew. Wagers were heavy that if she ever caught the big guy cheating in an obvious way, California would end up in the sea.

"I don't want the girl for sex."

"You'd better not," a female voice answered from seemingly nowhere.

Felipe practically jumped out of his skin and peered around.

Lucifer, on the other hand, didn't appear surprised at all. "Calm yourself, kitty. She's not here, but she's got eyes and ears everywhere. Can you believe she doesn't trust me?" Lucifer pretended affront then grinned. "Smart woman. Jealous woman too. I like that about her. Anyhow, we're getting off topic. I want you to go to Siren Isle and convince Jenny to join my legion of awesome minions."

"Me?"

"Yes, you. You have a way with ladies. I want you to use that famous charm, deviled tongue, magic dick, whatever it takes to get her back to the inner circle. If I weren't currently involved with a woman who doesn't understand how cruel monogamy is for a lusty man, I'd do it myself. But my girlfriend is a cruel mistress. Another thing that makes her unique and worth a little effort." Lucifer lowered his voice to a whisper. "Just don't tell her."

"I won't." Mostly because talking to Mother Nature was likely to rile Lucifer's jealous side and see him roasted over a low flame basted in his own juices.

"Smart kitty. So that's the plan. Travel there and do anything it takes to bring Jenny back to the castle. Oh, and be prepared to fight."

"I'm pretty sure I can handle one reluctant siren."

"She's not exactly a siren. No one's quite sure what she is as a matter of fact. And handling her won't be your biggest problem. Getting her off the island is."

"Am I going to have to fight the sirens to take her?" Because if that was the case, then he could run into a few problems. Very few males encountered those wenches and walked away— body and freewill intact. It took only a few notes, so he'd heard, to turn most males into mindless slaves. Good thing he was tone-deaf. He wouldn't know good music if it slapped him in the face with a guitar.

"Fight the sirens? I doubt it will come to that. While Thelxiope might have said I couldn't have Jenny, the other sirens all think it would be good for Jenny to expand her horizons. The problem is, whenever Jenny goes anywhere near the water, we have sea monster problems. As in, they go ballistic and won't let her leave."

"Can't the boatman beat them back with his oar?"

"That only works for Charon."

Felipe scrubbed his face, feeling whiskers pop as his inner kitty grew more and more agitated with the mission.

"Is she truly that necessary to the legion?"

"She has special skills I need."

"Can I ask what those skills are?" Felipe doubted they were the boudoir kind. Mother Nature had made it pretty clear what would happen if she caught Lucifer cheating on her. That woman wielded an evil green thumb when provoked.

"No, you may not ask."

"I guess saying I'm busy isn't an option?"

Lucifer smirked. "Depends. Are you attached to your fur? I could use a new rug for my office."

Forget hiding the shudder that went through him at the polite menace in his boss's voice. Felipe shivered and executed a salute for good measure. "It will be as you order, boss. I'll be leaving right away."

"I thought you might." A smug smile graced Lucifer's lips. "Now, if you'll excuse me, I'm late for lunch with Gaia, which means I'm going to get scolded." Lucifer rubbed his hands together. "I can't wait."

Again with the darned curiosity. "You want to fight with your girlfriend?"

"Of course I do. A big fight means make-up sex. The best kind. Some days it's good to be me." With a snap of his fingers, the Lord of Hell popped off leaving behind only a faint cloud of smoke reeking of brimstone.

Finished packing, Felipe swung his duffel bag over his shoulder. "I guess I'm going on a beach vacation."

On the bright side, he was pretty sure his rival Remy never boasted bedding a siren before. Maybe he could make this trip worth his while. As for the dark side of his quest? He didn't believe in negativity. He would prevail. He was a hellcat, and he always landed on his feet.

Chapter Three

Perched atop her assigned rock on the island's edge, Jenny combed out her corkscrewed, still green hair. At least she'd gotten past the point of wincing whenever she hit a snarled spot. Gallons of conditioner and habit meant she could now handle the daily torture. Raidne insisted she do it, even if her hair tangled within moments and the sailors never seemed impressed with her strange-colored locks. "Looks like moldy straw," more than one of them observed. And no amount of bleaching or hair products could change that fact. But at least it was soft, even if it always had a windblown appearance.

"I don't feel any vibrations," Raidne hollered, interrupting her rhythmic strokes.

Probably because Jenny wasn't singing yet. This was the part of her day she always dreaded. All the sirens on the Isle, even Jenny, the adopted, honorary one, took a turn crooning to the waves. Although, in Jenny's case it was less croon, more like croak, massacre, and torture anything with ears.

Despite all her lessons, everything Jenny uttered seemed to grate upon the listener. Nails on chalkboard couldn't compare with her voice.

Didn't stop her teachers from insisting she sing. They were convinced she held some siren root—a warped one—probably passed down through one of their rare male offspring sent off into the big world because Siren Isle catered to women only. Well, women, their children, and their captive lovers. Of which currently only lovers applied. The sirens hadn't sired any daughters in decades, centuries in the case of Thelxiope and Raidne. It wasn't for lack of trying, though.

Each of the sirens had their own harem of men, lovers whose sole purpose was to serve their mistress in whatever way she desired. They also made great maids and farmers when their boudoir talents weren't up to par or in need.

How Jenny sometimes envied them the extra helping hands. Poor Jenny had no sailors to do her bidding. Her one and only boyfriend was a courtesy one given to her by Molpe on her twenty-first birthday to take care of her virginity problem. He solved it all right, and she'd even grown fond of him and he of her until the idiot removed the wax plugs in his ears.

He couldn't swim away from the isle fast enough when he heard her truly sing for the first time. He didn't get far. The Styx harbored too many hungry denizens.

Heartbroken for a while, Jenny got over his loss, but she never accepted the offer of a replacement. If you asked her, sex was overrated. She much preferred a good book, but she did miss his mopping and dusting skills.

"Still not sensing any singing!" Raidne yodeled.

In spite of clearing the area before her open-air concerts, her teachers always knew. Apparently Jenny's special melodic talent caused a deep thrumming in the rocks lining the island. It also caused nosebleeds, deafness, madness, and screams for mercy from those unlucky enough to actually hear it.

Forget the usual tales of sirens and their lovely melodies luring sailors to their deaths or enslaving them to their will. Unlike her aunts who could charm a man into doing anything they wanted, when Jenny sang, things wanted to kill themselves.

And yet her adopted aunts all insisted she practice her corrupted talent.

"Jenny!" Raidne hollered her name.

No more putting it off. Time to pitch a note. Jenny's lips parted, and she sang. It didn't take long for the effect to show. A lone bird dropped from the sky with a warbling croak. The dancing waves that rolled onto the rocks on shore retreated. The sunlight from the mortal realm, which streamed through the odd hole in the clouds, dimmed.

Despite it all, once Jenny started, she relaxed. Smiled. Closed her eyes and, in her mind, to her own ears, heard only beauty.

A shame no one else did.

The screaming started about halfway through her seventh song.

"Make it stop!" a voice shrieked. "Please, by all that's unholy, make it stop singing."

Jenny cut off mid note in time to hear a smooth, masculine reply. "Shut up you, idiot. It's not that bad."

A brow arched of its own volition. *Not that bad?* She'd never heard anyone say that before. Even Molpe, the most patient of her teachers, couldn't hide a pained wince when Jenny went all out. While their siren attributes made them more or less immune to the effects of her voice, strong musical renditions tended to grate unpleasantly even for them.

Leaning forward on her perch, Jenny peeked over the edge of her rock. Below her was where the dock to the isle, the only safe spot to land, inched out into the bay where the Styx flowed on the one side, and the Darkling Sea buffeted from the other.

A long boat bobbed on the waves, one from Charon's fleet, similar to the one that had dumped those poor souls last week. Jenny still felt bad about what happened to them.

But as Aunt Raidne said to cheer her up, "Not your fault they got lost. Maybe next time Lucifer will keep better track of his recruits. And besides, having soul-zombies that don't leave icky body parts everywhere will only enhance our reputation, not to mention keep our beaches clean of corpses."

Raidne, always seeing the bright and disturbing side of things.

Back to the current boat. Were they here to herd the zombies back to the nine circles of Hell? Did they arrive here by accident?

And who was the tall, good-looking fellow with the deep black hair hued with hints of red and a muscular body usually seen only in Molpe's calendar of Chippenhell's Exotic Strippers? Jenny stared. She couldn't help it.

Most of the sailors who landed on the isle were bewitched by her aunts, pathetic in their eagerness, and mindless in their need to please, their lust was for the one who sang them to the isle's shores. Jenny's seamen, on the other hand, were usually crying for their mothers and rocking themselves while humming. It was hard to find a man attractive when he was drooling and staring off into space.

Yet, this fellow seemed unaffected by her singing, unlike his companion who held a rag to his bloody nose. *He must be wearing some new kind of protective ear gear.*

Whoever they were and whatever they wanted wasn't Jenny's problem. She called for her aunt. "We have visitors!"

The sailor, standing on unsteady legs and clutching at his oar, moaned and wavered while fresh blood ran from his nose. The man with the impressive physique didn't so much as shudder. On the contrary, he swiveled his head and glanced to her rocky aerie, caught her staring, and smiled. Full-lipped, white-toothed, and utterly beguiling.

Oh my. It was Jenny's turn for once in her life to suffer faint legs. She collapsed on her butt. Stunned. Slightly breathless. And warm all over.

What magic is this?

She didn't know why, but when a faint chuckle drifted to her on the briny breeze, her nipples hardened and she had to crawl from the edge, lest she give in to temptation and peek again.

She'd just reached the edge of her rock when Raidne appeared.

"Good grief, Jenny, why are you slithering about on the ground like a snake? You'll dirty your skirts."

"He smiled at me." Jenny stated it as if that were all the explanation needed.

All it did was confuse poor Raidne. "Who smiled at you?"

"The man on the dock. He smiled at me, and next thing I knew, I couldn't catch my breath and my legs went weak."

"Truly?" Raidne beamed. "This I have to see."

To Jenny's horror, her aunt strode to the edge. "Watch yourself, Aunt. He's got some powerful magic."

Ignoring her advice, Raidne stared down below. "And a really cute butt. Yoo-hoo, ahoy there, handsome."

"My lady of the isle, how kind of you to greet me," was the velvety, masculine reply.

Thank goodness Jenny was still on the ground because the sound of his voice made her shiver. Jenny waited for her aunt to collapse before his seductive magic. She didn't, but she did let out a low whistle of appreciation.

"He's also got an impressive set of abs. I think I should inspect those up close."

Raidne straightened and fluffed her bosom so it practically spilled out of her gown, smoothed down her skirts, and finger combed her long, blonde hair.

"Careful, Aunt. He's wearing some protective ear gear of some sort. My song didn't affect him."

"Don't worry about me, Jenny. Auntie will take care of the dashing young man." With a wink and a lick of her lips, Raidne skipped out of sight down the stone steps carved into the bluff.

Tummy still doing flips, Jenny debated heading back to her cave—decked out in the finest ornaments from wrecked sea-ships a girl could ask for—or keeping an eye on her aunt.

Oh, who am I kidding? I want to peek at that man again.

Back she crept to the edge of the cliff. She peered over the edge, met the bold stare of the newcomer, only inches from her face, and shrieked.

Chapter Four

The girl certainly has lungs. Felipe didn't quite wince, but it was close, especially since she uttered the shrill scream just inches from his ears.

"I guess I should excuse myself for startling you." A polite apology, something Lucifer would hate, but Felipe had learned over the years the value of a strategic excuse, especially where women were concerned.

"What did you do to my aunt?" she demanded, her voice a low, sultry buzz that, while not on the same songbird pleasant level of the woman who met him by the dock, actually made his inner kitty want to purr.

"Do you mean the blonde who came to greet me and the boatman?"

"Yes, her. What did you do to her?" she asked, a tiny line forming between her brows.

"Nothing. I just asked her if she could point me in the direction of one Jenny of the isle, and she told me to look up here."

"She did?" The girl blinked in surprise and moved away from the edge to sit on her haunches, her gown puddled in a heap around her.

Felipe used her momentary distraction to vault himself over the edge. The precarious stairs cut into the rock were more suited to a mountain goat or his hellcat shape than a man—no matter how nimbly the blonde siren skipped down them.

On even ground, he perused the chit before him. Unlike the voluptuous blonde siren who met him, this girl was … different. For one, her hair was a striated green color, ranging from a deep almost black green to a pale almost blonde. It hung in rumpled waves around her head and gave her the appearance of having just rolled out of bed—after a lively night of lovemaking. *Meow*.

Her skin was pale and almost pearl-like in its luminosity while her lips were the pink of rose petals. As for her eyes, they were the dark blue of a stormy sea and fixed on him with curiosity and suspicion.

He couldn't tell much about her shape other than she seemed to possess an impressive set of tits, the kind a man could bury his face in and blow satisfying raspberries. Overall, she was cute, and his inner kitty urged him to get closer, maybe rub against her and…

"What manner of ear protection are you wearing? I can't see it."

"I'm not wearing any." Because he'd learned by accident some time ago that the sirens' songs didn't affect him. Something he'd not mentioned to Lucifer when trying to back out of the mission, but which he suspected the Dark Lord already knew.

"You're not? And you can hear me?"

What an odd question. "Of course I can. Would we be having this conversation otherwise?"

"And you're sane?"

He couldn't help but chuckle. "I guess that depends on who you ask."

"I mean, you don't feel an urge to throw yourself off the cliff? Claw out your own eyes? Choke yourself? Jab needles in your ears?"

As her list went on and one, his eyes widened until with her, "Have an urge to eat brains?", he halted her. "Slow down, sweetheart. If you're asking if I have any suicidal, homicidal, or cannibalistic desires currently on my mind, then the answer is no."

She seemed even more flummoxed than before. "Not even one? You feel nothing?"

"Well, if you're asking how I feel, then I am a tad hungry. The culinary skills of the boatman left much to be desired. And maybe a touch tired." The sunlight called to his kitty to find a warm patch and curl up for a nap. He also didn't mention the slightly horny state he found himself in. That wasn't something any male blurted aloud unless drunk or in the company of nymphs. And even then, a male should be careful.

Arousal around any group of nymphs was akin to throwing a slab of steak to a hellhound after a day spent on patrol. You were likely to get devoured. You just might not survive it.

"This is incredible," she mumbled.

If she was talking about him, then yes, he'd have to agree. He would even love to show her. He bet her hair would look lovely fanned across a pillow with her skirts hiked high around those creamy, surely plump thighs of hers. Incredible wouldn't be the only word she'd use to describe him once he was done pleasuring her.

Slow down, kitty. Curtailing that line of thought, he brought himself back to the mission at hand. "As I said before, I'm looking for someone. A girl named Jenny. Do you know her?"

"Yes. Very well you could say." The pink lips curved.

His cock swelled and urged him to get closer, as in between her legs, skin-to-skin closer. *Down, boy.* Answers first, then seduction. "Is she nearby?"

"Closer than you'd expect." The girl leaned forward and stared at him. "You really aren't affected, are you?"

By her presence? Oddly enough yes. But he wasn't about to admit it. "No. Now, if you don't mind, much as I'm enjoying our conversation, I really need to find this Jenny person."

"What for?"

He bit back a sigh. "Because I need to talk to her."

"About?"

It might have taken him longer than it should have, but Felipe finally clued in. "You're Jenny, aren't you?"

"Maybe."

"Don't maybe me. Are you or aren't you?"

"I am. So now that you know, will you answer why you want me?"

I want you because you've got incredible lips, fascinating hair, and a mouth that really needs a set of lips, my lips actually, to stop the never-ending questions. He instead settled on, "I'm supposed to bring you back to the inner circle of Hell to meet with Lucifer."

He expected a few reactions—an adamant no, maybe more questions, possibly even tears begging him not to take her. What he got was laughter, a laughter that vibrated every one of his nerves, a laughter that had his inner feline rolling onto its back in ecstasy, purring, and an urge to drop to his knees and kiss the perfect, chuckling lips.

I'm bewitched!

Chapter Five

Of all the things she expected the handsome stranger to say, his wanting to escort her to meet with Lucifer wasn't on the list.

"I'm afraid you'll have to let me in on the joke because I don't get it," he said, interrupting her mirth with a grouchy query.

"Sorry. It's just you're the first person to ever come looking for me, which in and of itself is, well, kind of amazing. And then you tell me you want to take me to visit the Lord of the Pit." She shrugged. "I'm not even sure why that's funny. It just is. I mean, are you sure he said Jenny? There have got to be a lot of Jennys. What makes you think I'm the one?"

"Are there any other Jennys on the island?"

"No."

"Then you're the one."

Stranger and stranger, just like him. But that she could solve. "Who are you?"

"Felipe."

"That doesn't tell me much."

A wicked arch of one brow went well with the tilt of his lips. "Are we exchanging life histories? Fine. Here's mine in a nutshell. Orphaned as a cub, I was taken in by a kind witch who raised me as her beloved pet until I got old enough to get a job, find a place of my own, and move out. I enjoy getting drunk with my friends, wenching, getting into catfights and antagonizing hellhounds. In my spare time, I do work for

35

Lucifer, usually because I need to do something to get back in his good graces. I'm not much one for rules."

The more he spoke, the rounder her eyes surely grew. His story sounded fine except for one sticky part. "Beloved pet?" What woman would treat a child like that?

He chuckled. "Before you go getting the wrong idea, I guess I should mention I'm a shapeshifter. A hellcat to be precise."

"A cat? Really? Can I see?" She'd not gotten many chances to interact with animals given most of them died before she'd finished saying, 'Aren't you just the cutest thing.'

"Maybe later. We really should get moving if we don't want our boatman to sail away on the next tide without us."

"I'd worry more about my aunts adding him to their collection. Pickings have been slim lately. The Bermuda Triangle hasn't been sending as many ships this way as in the past. Apparently, the mortal realm sailors are getting better at avoiding it." The aunts had spoken a lot recently of either getting the interdimensional rip moved or having a new one created. They'd yet to progress past the talking stage since the creation of new tears in reality was costly and difficult.

"Then we should hurry."

"You expect me to rush off with you on the basis of your word without talking first to my aunts or packing anything?"

"Well, yeah. I mean, I kind of hoped." He shot her an engaging smile, and she almost found herself saying yes.

She frowned instead. "You say Lucifer sent you. He's the one in charge of Hell, right?"

"The one and only."

"How intriguing. My history lessons speak of the circles and their leader." But Jenny had found the subject dull and didn't pay much attention. Who cared about a place she'd never visit and a man she'd never meet? "What does he want me for?"

"He wouldn't say."

"Well, it doesn't really matter. Want me or not, even if I decided to go, I couldn't."

"Why not?"

"The monsters of the Styx and the Darkling Sea seem to take issue with me leaving the isle. The last time I attempted to go for a boat ride, they sank us less than a league out." For some reason, Jenny was confined to the island. The other sirens could come and go as they pleased, but Jenny? For all intents and purpose, Jenny was a prisoner.

"I am aware of your dilemma. That's why Lucifer sent me. You could say the beasts in the river and I have an understanding."

"You can speak to them?"

"More like eat them, but since they both have to do with my mouth, I'd say they're close enough to be considered the same." His lips split in a wide smile, which showcased a mischievous dimple. "So, what do you say? Are you coming with me?"

Jenny's tummy did that funny thing again. Supper must approach.

Leave? Leave the one place that accepted her for who she was, whatever she was? Frightening and exciting all at the same time. "I need time to think about it, and speak to my aunts."

"But the boat—"

"Will be fine, as will your pilot," Raidne said, interrupting them. She crested the cliff, skirts held in one hand, displaying her rounded calves. "He's not my type anyhow. Why don't you follow Jenny back to her cave and spend the night? We can gather in the morning to discuss your plans."

Jenny practically squeaked in shock. Her aunt wanted her to take this virtual stranger to her home, alone. What if he attempted to ravish her or something? *I should be so lucky.*

"I guess spending one night wouldn't hurt. Lead the way, ladies."

Linking her arm through Jenny's, Raidne led the way, hips swinging, skirts swishing. Casting a less-than-discreet glance over shoulder, Jenny noted Felipe followed at a slower pace, taking in the islands sights. Facing forward again, Jenny hissed, "What's going on?"

"Whatever do you mean, dear child?"

"Don't dear child me. Not your type? So long as they're still breathing any man is your type, and I thought our caves were off limits to men. Isn't that what the love shacks are for?" And, yes, that was as tawdry as it sounded. Ensorcelled prisoners were given little cabanas, which basically consisted of a large bed and washroom facilities. While sirens had uses for men, it didn't extend to companionship outside the bedroom.

"Our new friend here isn't a conquest but a guest. Guests are treated differently."

"I wouldn't know. We've never had a male guest before."

Raidne's lip curled with disdain. "Because our usual visitors lack balls. But not this Felipe fellow. He's got a strong will to go with his big muscles. A shame we can't play with him."

"Why not?" Jenny had never known the sirens to abstain from anyone before.

"You heard the man. Lucifer wants you."

"And for that reason alone, Felipe is off limits?"

"All of Lucifer's special soldiers are, even we are not so foolish as to cross the Dark Lord. And messing with one of his minions on a mission would definitely accomplish that."

"So why even the pretense of discussion? If you're so scared of him, then why aren't I already sailing away?"

"Because, dear child, one doesn't simply give in at the first request. Have we taught you nothing? Always play hard to get. Find out as much as you can before you gracefully give in."

"Find out what, though? Felipe has already stated he doesn't know what Lucifer wants me for."

"Yet, it must be important because, despite Thelxiope telling him no over the phone, he felt a need to dispatch one of his more accomplished and handsome minions to complete the task."

"You mean you already know of Lucifer's demand for my presence?"

"Oh, did we forget to mention it? Yes, we were aware and, of course, answered on your behalf. Thelxy told him no."

"I'm confused. Didn't you just say you shouldn't cross him?"

"Yes, but as I also said, we couldn't just say yes. It would set a bad precedence. We do have a reputation to maintain. And I think Thelxy

39

was kind of hoping to goad the Dark One to pay us a visit in person. The man is a veritable machine in the bedroom, and his stamina…" Raidne let out a dreamy sigh. "But ever since he hooked up with that goody two shoes, Gaia, he no longer plays the field. He's now monogamous. Who would have thought we'd ever see the day when the world's most renowned player would tether his balls."

When it came to lovers, the sirens held the opinion variety was best. "Can we get back on track instead of discussing your sex life?"

"If you insist, although I personally think my coital pursuits are of more interest than a short phone call. Lucifer called. Asked if he could borrow you. Big sis said no, I said maybe, Lucifer said he'd send a man, end of story."

"No, not end of story. Why is it no one thought to ask me?"

"Do you want to go?"

Jenny's first impulse was to say no. The island was all she knew. Her aunts the only ones to not run and scream when she spoke. Or were until Felipe came along. Were there more people like him in the nine circles of Hell? Could she explore past her current boundaries and see what else life had to offer a girl who was neither mermaid nor siren?

"I wouldn't be averse to seeing the world a bit."

"Then it's settled. You can leave in the morn with the handsome cat."

Trust her aunt to make it seem so simple. "But what of the Styx monsters? You know they won't let me leave."

"The hellcat seems to think he can get past them."

"And if he's wrong?"

Raidne shrugged. "Then he'll get eaten. Really, Jenny, you need to stop with the pessimism. I know your life here isn't all you could wish. Can you really tell me you're not tempted to take a chance and go with the young fellow and see what Lucifer wants? What lies beyond our rocky shores?"

Raidne's observation so closely mirrored her own thoughts that she could almost wonder if she'd read her mind. *Or just understands me better than I give her credit for.*

Ever since her abandonment, Jenny struggled with trust. While her adopted aunts had welcomed her with open arms, she feared one day they too would drug her and dump her, no longer willing to deal with her flaws. *If my own mother couldn't love me, then how can I expect anyone else to?*

"Hey," Raidne whispered against her ear. "Don't turn around, but I do believe the handsome cat is checking out your ass."

He was what? Despite being told not to, Jenny's head swiveled, and indeed, she caught Felipe, a few yards behind, staring unabashedly. At least she assumed he felt no shame, given the wide smile and wink he tossed her.

Cheeks flaming, she quickly turned away, but she couldn't stop her racing pulse. Why did he have such an effect on her? What did it mean? Would it get worse?

I hope not because I am taking him to my cave, and I really don't want to embarrass myself. By all the sand in the ocean, she hoped she'd not left any underwear on the floor.

Chapter Six

The mission certainly had taken an entertaining twist. It seemed his hostesses were unaware this hellcat possessed excellent auditory senses, which meant he heard every word of their interesting conversation. Enlightening, and hopeful. It seemed Jenny wanted to leave with him. She just harbored a few minor doubts. Doubts he'd work at putting at ease. After all, convincing ladies to give in to his whims was a specialty of his.

He was quite surprised at the hospitality offer, almost as much as Jenny was. He'd heard rumors of the way things worked around here. Siren Isle had quite the reputation. Lured men were used as studs and while they guested—in some cases for life—were kept segregated from the sirens, their daughters, and any other female guests. To call this place matriarchal was an understatement. The sirens truly had no use for males other than their cocks and semen—the creamy kind, not the sailing kind.

To have one of the original sirens, or so legend had it—the legend speaking of four sisters born of some sort of ocean god—invite him to stay with a protégé of theirs was frankly unheard of. Which meant he'd better tread carefully. While he might find himself attracted to the green-haired chit, this was one time when seduction might serve to make things more deadly rather than less.

Knowing this didn't stop him from checking out her plump ass that wiggled as she walked ahead or him tossing her his best panty-dropping grin when she caught him peeking. The red in her cheeks surprised him. Sirens weren't known for their shy and virginal responses.

The trail they followed proved pleasant, lined with bushes and foliage boasting giant colorful blooms with exotic fragrances. While not quite paved, it was close, with seashells pounded into the ground to give it a cobbled feel. The usual symphony of birds, natural to most jungle habitats didn't exist here, and he briefly wondered at the lack. Actually, there was a lack of any animal life; no drone of insects or rustling of leaves as something small and furry skittered away. Stretching his senses, he sniffed, and his kitty seemed flummoxed at the lack of scent from anything it considered prey.

The strange hole in the ash clouds allowed a beam of pure sunlight through, the how and why a mystery as far as Felipe knew. Some legends said it was the remnant of an ancient spell, cast by a mighty wizard to please his siren lover. Others that it was a hole in the hellzone atmosphere caused by too much cleanliness. Whatever the cause, the warm rays were pleasant, especially for someone who'd only very, very rarely been granted permission to visit the mortal side.

As to their destination, it wasn't hard to figure out. A massive cone-shaped mountain rose from the center of the island, an old volcano by its appearance, with frozen black streams of rock twisting and lumping down its sides and crisscrossed with more seashell paths leading to dark openings.

Fuck me, they are taking me to a cave. He'd hoped they joked. When the path split at the base of the mountain, the ladies halted, and Raidne kissed Jenny noisily on both cheeks whispering— but not low enough for him to miss—"Don't do anything I wouldn't."

"That's not a long list."

"Exactly," Raidne replied with a husky chuckle. To him she said, "Watch yourself, cat. You are a guest only so long as you behave. Step out of line, and minion on a mission or not, we'll have your heart for breakfast. Roasted and sliced on crackers with a smear of caviar."

Mmm, if it weren't his organ she spoke of, the snack would have sounded great.

With a smile and blown kiss of goodbye, the siren who'd just threatened him literally, skipped off while humming.

"That is one seriously freaky lady." He'd not realized he spoken aloud until Jenny said, "Yes, she is. And even better, she means every word."

So not reassuring.

Turning to his hostess for the night, Felipe tried to veer the conversation to something less disturbing than the image of a beautiful woman with cannibalistic natures. "Where are we going?"

"My home. It's up this way. I chose a cave toward the top of the volcano because I enjoy the view of the ocean, especially when a storm rolls in."

Holding aloft her skirts with one hand, and showing off trim calves covered in an odd pattern of green scales that shimmered in the light, she nimbly skipped along the steep trail. Felipe had to hurry to keep pace. She'd not kidded when she said the top. Good thing he kept fit or he would have found himself huffing and puffing when they finally reached the aerie's entrance. That kind of external manifestation of exertion was only acceptable when naked and fucking. Other than that, a male had to maintain the appearance of being a big, tough bastard— even if inside he was a pussy cat.

In front of the gaping maw, which he assumed served as her front door, was a wide-open space, a patio of sorts. It featured, of all things, a pair of chairs, one an Adirondack, the other a carved wooden rocker, both facing the horizon.

Felipe paused to gape. "You weren't kidding about the view." Magnificent didn't come close to describing it. The dark waves of the Darkling Sea rolled, the crests of some peaks frothing white, the dark and light contrasting with the reddish hue of Hell's skyline.

Jenny turned a dreamy gaze outward. "Pretty, isn't it? I love to sit out here and watch it, imagining."

"Imagining what?"

"Nothing a man like you would find interest in," was her curt reply as she spun away and led the way into the dark hole cut in the mountainside.

Felix truly didn't want to follow. He really didn't enjoy confined spaces. Couldn't he remain outside in the fresh air where there was plenty of space? He could sleep in the chair. He didn't mind. He'd slept in worse spots in the past—the cat carrier Ysabel stuffed him in whenever they traveled came to mind.

Remaining outside, though, smacked too much of cowardice, and besides, he didn't want Jenny to have time to change her mind. *Keep 'em off balance so they don't know what hit him*, an expression Lucifer liked to use and that, oddly enough, worked most of the time.

Be a man and not a fraidy cat. With a scowl, and a curse for the demon lord who made him do the most annoying things, Felipe followed. Into the belly of darkness he strode, walked a few yards, stopped dead, and stared, utterly stunned. "I have to admit I wasn't expecting this."

People heard the words, "lives in a cave" and immediately the image conjured involved rough walls, a dirt floor, stalactite ceiling, oh and the kind of cold and damp that made you wish for sunshine.

In this case, the only part that applied to his predefined notions was cave. Yes, they'd entered a giant hole in a volcano and walked a few feet down a hallway with smooth walls except for the glittering line of seashells embedded in it. The tunnel opened into a large cavern, like majorly large, with a ceiling that domed high overhead.

And this was where his perceptions had to shift. The stone might have proven cold if not for the myriad rugs covering the space, from the massive oriental one set between a pair of almost matching blue couches to the rag-tiled oval contoured one under a carved wooden dining set to the cream-colored shag nestled alongside the four-poster bed.

I wonder if I'll get to sink my toes into that in the morning. Guess it depends on where I'm sleeping tonight and with whom.

A massive flat screen television hung above a fireplace. Within the massive stone-carved hearth, flames danced and crackled while sconces lit the space with a warm glow from their evenly spaced positions on the walls.

An open kitchen area was set against the rear wall boasting stainless steel appliances, driftwood cupboards, and a massive island, the granite top alone bigger than his bed at home.

"Nice place," he uttered, even if it seemed inadequate. The girl was living in the lap of luxury. No wonder she seemed hesitant to leave it all behind. Heck, he'd show reticence too given space went for a premium especially in the inner ring of Hell.

"Thanks," Jenny said, not meeting his eyes. "Most of it we salvaged from the ships that wash against the rocks."

Less wash and more like crashed. "The water doesn't ruin it?" he asked vaguely, gesturing to the television.

"Depends on if we get to the wreck before it sinks."

"What do you do with the extra stuff?"

"My aunt Teles manages an online Helliji account where she auctions off the items we don't need or she barters it for stuff we want. We're not exactly on any trade routes, so getting essentials takes a bit of work."

"And this is all yours?"

"Yes. It's not as big or opulent as my aunts places, but I like the cozy atmosphere."

He almost choked at her use of the word cozy. Cozy was his one-room bachelor pad with its Murphy bed which, when in its upright position, allowed him to use the built-in drawers for storage and had a drop-down shelf with a cushion for a couch. Felipe could have afforded a bigger place, but didn't bother. He rarely spent time at home, preferring to roam and get into trouble. Or spend his nights in someone else's bed.

"Are you hungry?" she asked as she left his side to enter the kitchen area. Opening the fridge, she began to pull out food, which she placed on the island, a heap of vegetables he noted with a wrinkle of his nose.

"Yes."

"How do you feel about seafood?" she asked, turning to finally face him.

"Love it. Do sirens eat it?" Or did they consider them family? Wait, he was mixing them up with mermaids.

There was a misconception in the mortal realm about sirens and mermaids being one and the same. Hardly. Sirens, who were more closely related to birds than aquatic creatures, lived on land and collected what they needed from the ocean. They looked and lived like humans, except for the fact they aged very slowly, could sing a man into doing whatever they wanted, oh and were cold-blooded killers.

Mermaids, on the other hand, were half woman, half fish, living under the waves of the ocean. They, too, took their bounty from the sea and were also cold-blooded killers, but they didn't use song to achieve their goal. Their methods were more savage. His one encounter with a mermaid who'd accidentally ended up in the Styx didn't leave him with an urge to meet one again.

"Of course they eat fish, as do I."

"You speak as if you're not one of them?"

She rolled her shoulders. "I'm not technically."

"But you live here and call them all aunt."

"Only because of circumstance." When she would have stopped there, he stared at her pointedly until she continued. "My turn to spill my life story, I take it? It's not very interesting. I was abandoned here by my mermaid mother when I was young. The sirens felt sorry for me and took me in to raise as one of their own. They seem to think my affliction might be siren-based."

"What affliction?"

From where he sat, Felipe noted no imperfection. On the contrary, Jenny possessed an exotic beauty that he'd rarely encountered, a wild purity he found insanely attractive. Just ask his semi-erect cock and his inner kitty, which would have loved a chance to lick her with a raspy tongue from head to toe.

"Well, in case you hadn't noticed, I don't have a fish tail. Which was quite embarrassing to my mother who was considered to have one of the more beautiful ones in her school."

"I thought I heard mermaids were all women, which means the fathers are—"

"All human or, in some rare cases, demons. But the only thing we usually inherit from our fathers is their eyes. Mermaids give birth to the next generation. Which means tails and seaweed hair."

"Your hair is green," he pointed out.

"But it's hair that set me apart. Then there was the whole can't-breathe-underwater thing."

"So you're different. That's still not a reason for a mother to abandon you." He found his temper rousing for her, angered that anyone could abandon their child over small things that shouldn't matter.

"Oh, I'm sure if it had just been that, she might have kept me, but then there was the biggest problem of all. When I speak or sing, things either die, maim, or kill themselves. Something about my voice sets them off."

Other than a huskiness and tenor a touch lower than most women, he'd not noticed an issue with her speech. He actually thought it was kind of sexy. "It doesn't bother me."

"So I've noted. And you've no idea why?"

"No."

"A shame," she said with a sigh as she withdrew a wickedly long knife and began expertly chopping her pile of vegetables.

"Why a shame?"

She threw him a pointed look. "Did you not hear what I just said? People freak when I speak. And when I sing, I can literally kill."

"If you ask me, that's a pretty cool power. A lot less messy than what I have to do to get some respect. Breaking out the claws to mete out some justice and a lesson in manners means getting blood on my fur and sometimes cracking a nail."

"So you take a bath. I don't see the big deal. At least you have the choice of who gets hurt."

"Did you just tell me to take a bath?" He didn't have to pretend affront. Did she truly know nothing about his kind? "I'm a cat, woman! The only time we go near water is to hunt. And even then, we prefer to lure our aquatic snacks to a shallow place where we can grab them and drag them to shore."

"If you don't bathe, then how do you stay clean?" she asked with a cute wrinkle of her nose.

"When I'm in my human shape, I can handle a shower. It's when I'm not that I run into issues."

"So what do you do?"

"For one, I try to stay out of messy situations. But when I can't avoid them, and I get some blood or something else on my precious feline's fur, then I'm licking for hours. Which, I might add, is not much fun. Do you know how gross it is to hack up hairballs?" Felipe shuddered. "Not to mention it clogs the pipes when I spit them out in the sink."

It started with a shake of her frame, a tremble, then turned into full-on laughter.

"It's not funny," he stated in mock affront.

"Oh yes it is," she said in between chuckles. "I'd take hairballs and clogged plumbing over more damned roasted seagull for dinner any day. The sirens hate to see things go to waste, so whenever I'd play outside and got too noisy, we'd end up with whole flocks of visiting seagulls dropping dead."

"Is that why there are no birds on the island?"

"Partially. But, even before my arrival, there was little alive on this island other than the sirens and their captives. I asked Raidne about it once, but she couldn't explain why. While we can maintain aquariums, anything else just ends up dying."

"So no steak? Or venison or mice?"

"Nope, not unless we salvaged some from a wreck. But we do have lots of fresh seafood." She no sooner said this than she open a cupboard door in the island, stuck her hand in, and withdrew it, holding a massive, mottled green/brown lobster. "Would you like butter sauce with it?"

Would he ever.

A while later, his belly full, and utterly content—the green-haired Jenny could cook!—Felipe finally voiced the question plaguing him. "Tell me to mind my business if you want, but I have to ask. If your mother didn't want to keep you, then why not send you to live with your father?" As soon as he said it, he wanted to take it back, especially since he couldn't miss the flash of sadness that hit her eyes. "I'm sorry. That was too personal," he quickly added.

"No. It's okay. I mean it's natural to wonder I guess. You do know mermaids are all female, right? Like sirens, they require humanoid males to beget children."

"Yeah, I'd heard, but how does that work? I mean you'd think their, um, plumbing wouldn't be compatible."

Laughter crinkled the corners of her eyes, and her lips took on a delightful smile he would have loved to kiss. "They're not, in their sea state. Which is why there are dry caves at the bottom of the ocean. Mermaids snatch drowning sailors and bring them to these air pockets and keep them as their mates. When the tide is high, if a mermaid allows her tail to dry, then for a little while, she appears completely human."

"And babies arrive nine months later."

"If lucky, the mermaids get pregnant and give birth to a new mermaid. Or at least that's what is supposed to happen. It didn't in my case."

"You took after your father and came out too human."

"Maybe."

"What do you mean, maybe?"

"My mother never said who my father was. She left the school one day to explore the ocean. When she returned, she was heavy with child and wouldn't say who got her that way. When I was born in the ocean, I almost drowned before they realized I didn't have gills. For years, my deformity meant I had to live in the caves. I guess the shame proved too much for my mother. One day, I went to sleep, and the next time I woke, I was sitting on the shore of Siren Isle."

A child abandoned and orphaned, kind of like him. Her story echoed his in many ways, except Felipe's mother had loved him until something bigger and badder killed her. He'd lucked out when Ysabel found him as a kitten and took him in, just like Jenny had with the sirens who'd adopted her.

"Have you ever tried to contact your mother to find out why? Maybe she had a good reason?"

"Nope. Nor do I intend to. I much prefer living here on the isle with the sunshine and acceptance than in the dark caverns where I was constantly belittled."

"I can't blame you. I'm a daylight-loving kind of guy myself, even if my usual sunshine is the bright glow of Hell's sky."

Curled up on the couch across from him, Jenny presented a pretty sight. At ease, her green locks tumbled around her tucked knees in tempting waves. Felipe couldn't recall a more relaxing evening, and, odder, he spent it conversing with someone of the opposite sex. Usually his conversation with women was short and to the point along the lines of "My place or yours?" and "Let's get naked." But with Jenny, he quite enjoyed learning about her, and, in an unusual twist, he imparted personal details about himself.

"What's Hell like?" she asked, interrupting his musing.

"What's Hell like?" he repeated. "Depends on which part of it. In the inner circle, things tend to remain orderly. Lucifer might like the results of chaos, and the sin revolving around it, but he doesn't enjoy living with it. Only his most trusted minions and allies are allowed to live in the inner ring. It's the least decayed of all the civilized zones. The streets are swept clean of ash numerous times a day, and Lucifer's guard keeps the criminal types in line. But the farther you move out, especially once you reach the fourth and fifth rings, the more society degrades. It gets harder to impose civilized rules, and the living conditions aren't exactly as favorable." Skirmishes broke out often as the damned and demons jostled for position and power. Buildings, no matter how new or renovated, aged quickly, an odd symptom of Hell that meant the construction and renovation business always had work.

"It sounds fascinating, but frightening at the same time."

"It is. But even amidst the ugly, there's beauty to be found. I once heard the Dark Lord say, how would we recognize perfection if it were not for the flaws that highlight it? In a sense, Hell does exactly that."

"An interesting perception."

"Apt as well. Does your curiosity about Hell mean you're willing to return with me?"

"Yes. No." She shrugged. "You're asking me to make a life-changing decision. It requires thought."

"If you say so. I see it more like an adventure."

"And let me guess, you always jump at the chance to experience new things?"

"All the time."

"And how has that worked for you?" she asked.

"I'm still alive, aren't I?" was his reply. He didn't mention the close calls and loss of a few of his nine lives. Curiosity was a dangerous thing.

"Do you think I'd fit in?" she asked, twirling a strand between her fingers.

Would she? Jenny possessed a purity to her that Hell often lacked. Not to say all its denizens were out-of-control murdering thugs, but they weren't in Hades because they'd lived a one hundred percent pristine life. Then again, some came close. Heaven's rules of entry went past strict on to ridiculous at times. But that wasn't her question. "I think the rings have a place for everyone, even a mermaid who can't swim."

"I can swim," she retorted. "Just not for long underwater."

"So you're no good at holding your breath."

"I bet I can hold it longer than you."

"Prove it," was the only warning he gave her before his tomcat impulse finally overrode his common sense. Before she could ask him what he meant, he'd landed on her couch, pulled her onto his lap, and devoured her luscious lips, stealing all her breath.

What he didn't expect was for her to steal his control.

Chapter Seven

Jenny had kissed a man before. She'd had the one boyfriend, after all, to experiment with. With all too much clarity, she recalled his sloppy embraces, the mashing and odd sensation of mouths pressed together.

That experience? Nothing compared to the embrace with Felipe.

One touch, just one, and her whole body ignited with heat. One firm slide of his lips on hers, and moisture rushed to her most private place, and a throb started within. His tongue flicked at the seam of her lips, and, instead of wanting to pull away, her breath stuttered, her mouth parted, and she clutched tight at his shoulders.

When he slid his tongue into her mouth, gliding it along her own, a moan sounded. *Was that me?* Indeed it was, just like it was her squirming on his lap, her sex aching for something. Something he understood and could give her.

A distinctly male hand, not that of a boy but calloused and sure, crept up her thigh, dragging her skirts with it. Cool air caressed her bare skin. Deft fingers kneaded her flesh. A warm, wet mouth did decadent things to her own. An oddly compelling need built within her.

Knuckles brushed the top of her mound, teasing. They returned, lower. The tip of a finger lightly skimmed across her clit. Again. Her breath caught as Felipe teased her with feather-light strokes.

A deep rumbling vibrated. Shook her. Was he … purring?

Shocked, she opened her eyes and found him staring at her, his eyes bright yellow and glowing, the hunger in them all too apparent. The grumbling purr came from him, from his feline side. And it struck her then in that moment how different he was from the men she'd met before.

A stranger. A stranger who was taking liberties with her body. Pleasurable ones, but still, Jenny couldn't help but wonder at how quickly she'd forgotten herself at his touch.

With a gasp, she leapt from his lap, her skirts tumbling back down to cover her throbbing sex. But she couldn't hide the fullness of her lips, the flush in her cheeks, or the racing of her pulse.

"You shouldn't have done that."

"Why not?"

"Because. We hardly know each other."

"We would have before the night was over, and quite intimately too," he drawled before curving his lips into a mischievous grin.

"I don't know what kind of magic you're using on me, but it needs to stop."

"No magic. Just pure unadulterated attraction."

"I am not attracted to you." Lie. She was. But Teles always taught her to never admit the truth unless it was to her advantage.

"I think I just proved otherwise, or would you like me to show you again?"

Yes please. She retreated a step, and he laughed, a low husky sound that skated along her exposed skin leaving goose bumps behind. And not the frightened kind.

"Stop that."

"Stop what?" he asked as he rose from the couch.

"Whatever you're doing."

"I'm showing my appreciation for a beautiful woman. What's wrong with that?"

He thinks I'm beautiful? Liar! His words dunked her in a cold shower of reality. "You're doing this because you think it will convince me to go with you. Well, you can stop. You don't need to fake or pretend interest in me. If I go, it will be because I want to and not because of your skills as a lover."

"You think I'm faking it?" His tone and raised brow of surprise seemed real, but Jenny was well aware of her shortcomings.

"Oh please. Are you going to tell me a man like yourself is overcome with lust by the sight of me? I do own a mirror you know." For years Jenny had the time to compare herself against the perfect beauty of her aunts. Beside their golden splendor and different, but shapely, figures, she was a pale, freakish-looking imitation. Everything about her was slightly off, from her voice to her strange hair to her overly wide hips and bosom and even her pale skin, which refused to tan even the slightest bit. Oh, and how about the fact her legs were covered in shiny scales?

Her only boyfriend had to be enchanted by her aunt to pay her any mind, and yet Felipe expected her to believe he was beset with desire for her? Ha. She wasn't that gullible. If her own mother couldn't see something to love, then how could a perfect stranger?

"I think it's time I went to bed," she announced.

"Great idea."

"Alone," she added pointedly.

"Ah, but my kitty loves to cuddle."

How a grown man could look so cute pouting, she couldn't have said. All she knew was it required more strength of will than she would have credited to shake her head. After that, she didn't say a word. She'd already spoken more in that one day than she ever recalled, the novelty of someone who could not only listen but pretended interest, and who wasn't one of the aunts, a joy she'd not expected.

Was it possible she could find more people who could tolerate her voice in Hell? She wondered as she ignored his teasing smile, a smile she aimed for when she tossed him a pillow and a blanket. Could she forge a new life, a different life for herself in the rings? She pondered those questions as she pointed to the couch while ignoring his moue of disappointment.

Did she have the courage needed to even attempt to leave the island? Even if they could make it past the Styx monsters, could she start over?

Maybe.

But … she was scared. *I don't want to be alone again.* She'd spent most of her early childhood virtually that way. What if she went to Hell and found herself shunned again?

Then I could always come back. The aunts loved her, even grumpy Thelxiope. But what if the lover she yearned for, the one man who would accept her for who she was, never wrecked upon the shores? Would she die alone? Or could she find the courage to perhaps seek out happiness? Yes, she might fail, but she could also find great happiness. Either way, she would never know unless she tried.

And on that note, she went to sleep, certain she couldn't ignore the fact the sexiest man ever slept only feet away, yet she did manage to slip into a deep slumber.

A pleasant dream where she ran through the mossy meadow on the isle while a giant kitty chased her. A single pounce was all it took for him to knock her down, gently, onto the spongy surface. Sitting atop her, his weight crushing, his slimy tongue laved her face with cold, wet strokes while cold air—

Jenny awoke suddenly only to realize her dream wasn't quite gone. Something did press on her chest, and something wet covered her mouth, preventing her from screaming. Eyes wide, she peered in the darkness, seeing only a vague shape hovering over her, a shape that wasn't Felipe and stank something fierce.

Death, decay, rotted fish, and stagnant seaweed. Whatever the scent truly was comprised of, it didn't matter. All Jenny knew was it didn't belong in her cave, she didn't want it touching her, and she certainly wasn't going to leave with it willingly.

Gross or not, she bit down on the flesh covering her mouth, and as the thing let out a pained grunt, she screamed.

And she didn't scream alone.

Chapter Eight

Felipe never slept heavily. He was a cat, AKA a predator, and the first rule any killer with an instinct for self-preservation learned was always keep one eye open, lest something bigger and badder come along and decide you'd make a tasty dinner. Or an awesome fur coat, which, given the rarity of his fur, was an attempt made more often than he liked.

Thus, when the shadowy figures, stinking of fish left out in the open air too long, drifted into the cave, bypassing his makeshift bed to where Jenny slept, he went on instant alert.

What the hell are these things? Definitely not dinner. He preferred his sushi more fresh smelling. Not friend because friends usually knocked and didn't arrive furtively under the cover of darkness. And he highly doubted they meant well. Call it instinct, or the obvious.

Careful to only move once the last one slipped past, Felipe adopted a kneeling position on the couch and peered over its back. With his enhanced eyesight, which had no issues seeing even in this murky dark, he noted a quad of creatures surrounded the bed. Of more interest, they seemed utterly oblivious to his presence, which meant they probably lacked a sense of smell. No creature with any kind of nose would have ignored the scent of cat permeating the place. He'd wager a further guess, judging by their wet appearance, that they were water based and up to no good.

Crouched on the couch, he planned his next move. Only idiots boldly rushed in. And Felipe didn't still own at least seven of his nine lives because he lacked wits. He took careful note of their weapons. They each bore deadly black blades, long and jagged edged, not made of steel according to the lack of gleam, but still solid appearing enough. He also observed their webbed fingers ended in claws, with hooks, which he discovered as one of them drew back the sheet covering Jenny. Sweet, defenseless Jenny wearing only a thin nightgown to cover her delicate skin. She shivered in the cool air, and a spark of irritation lit within Felipe.

How dare they disturb her sleep?

How dare they look upon her at all? snarled his cat.

His small ember of ire grew as one of them braced an arm over her chest and covered her mouth with a hand.

He's touching her. It wasn't just the man who didn't like that. His kitty took offense too.

Time for a midnight snack.

Before Felipe could spring into action, the creature holding Jenny yanked back his hand with a pained grunt, and Jenny uttered a scream that made even him wince. Gods, the girl, who was neither siren nor mermaid, could make herself heard. It set the dark figures around her yelling as they clapped hands to the stubby ears they bore on the sides of their heads.

Springing to her feet on the mattress, Jenny yodeled again as she kicked the one nearest to her in the face. Of course, her bare foot probably suffered more damage than the creature, or so he surmised by her cursing—a very colorful stream of words to make even the most seasoned sailor blush.

"Let go of me, you putrid sushi rejects," she hollered, kicking out at their lashing hands. She hopped around the bed avoiding their lunges, and Felipe jolted himself from the role of observer to action hero—or should he say kitty?—to the rescue.

Thankfully, Felipe always slept in the nude—a fact Jenny failed to notice given she never once looked his way once she went to bed.With a roar, he split his skin and let his fur pop through. Fangs descended. His body mass almost tripled in size. It took only a moment to exchange his male shape for that of his hellcat, but a moment was all the enemy needed to finally notice him and turn their attention from Jenny.

Excellent. *Come play with someone more your size.*

Hind legs bunched and pushed, propelling him off the couch to land in front of one of the monsters from the deep.

"Meowr!" he snarled.

"Blurgh!" yelled the beast.

And with their challenge uttered, they engaged. Four to one. Great odds. Felipe lashed with his heavy paws, claws out, and left a row of gouges across the torso of one. The wound oozed sluggish black blood, but it didn't slow the creature down.

From behind, another thought to attack, but his tail, which Felipe swore had a mind of its own, lashed the enemy much like a whip, the barb on the end catching and snagging a chunk of flesh, a sensitive part he'd wager judging by the bellow.

To his surprise, Jenny wasn't screaming anymore like most women would do if attacked in their sleep by a bunch of monsters. On the contrary, once she found a light switch and flicked it on, bathing them all in brilliance that had them all blinking for a second, she shouted encouragement.

"Kick him in the balls," she screeched. "Tear out his eyes. Rip off his arm. Stomp his toes." Blood-thirsty requests that he did his best to accommodate, a task made easier every time Jenny spoke. With every word she uttered, the creatures grew weaker, possibly because they bled from the ears and, in some cases, the two slits that passed for a nose. Jenny's special power at work.

Felipe had just finished slitting the throat of the last one when a commotion behind him drew his attention. He whirled to see one of the sirens standing there with a gleaming pitchfork, the tips of the tines covered in gore.

"What in Neptune's beard is going on?" she exclaimed.

"Aunt Teles! I was attacked."

"So I see. But it looks like it's been taken care of by your guest."

Since his kitty no longer seemed needed, Felipe pulled on his other shape, bones popping and fur shedding until he stood there in the flesh. Bare flesh.

From behind him, Jenny gasped, and from in front, Teles grinned. "Judging by his equipment, I'd say your cat is capable of taking care of more than just a few Undines."

"Aunt! Mind your manners," said a shocked Jenny.

"What? Was it something I said?" The sparkling mirth in Teles eyes let Felipe know she did it on purpose to tease Jenny.

He decided to save the more delicate sensibilities of his green-haired temptress—with the delectable potty mouth. He grabbed his jeans, which he'd draped over the couch earlier, and slipped them on, even as he tried to ignore the bits of blood and gore sticking to him from the fight.

"Are you all right?" A tentative touch had him slowly turning, but not slow enough. Jenny yanked back her hand as if burned.

"Perfectly fine. And you? You're not harmed?"

She shook her head. "No. I woke up before they could do anything, and then you took care of them."

"With some help. I saw you kick one in the face. How's your foot?"

She shrugged. "A little sore. But I'll be fine. I heal fast."

Teles snorted. "Fast is an understatement. Now that we've ascertained everyone is just peachy keen, how about we go and check on the others?"

"Where are the other aunts?" Jenny asked, a frown knitting her brow.

"It seems your cave wasn't the only thing attacked. Several quads of Undines invaded the isle. It is my regret to inform you, giant kitty, that one set unfortunately killed your boatman and sank his vessel."

"Charon is going to be pissed," Felipe muttered. "He's already paying an absurd insurance premium for my trip out here."

"Not as peeved as Thelxiope will be when she discovers they also took out the entire dock area. It took us years to build the last one to withstand the storms. She is going to have a fit when she finds out."

Jenny winced. "Not another mini hurricane. The last one totally messed up the gardens."

As they spoke, they made their way down the volcano, the low glow of solar lights, shaped like tiki torches, illuminating their way.

"So how many of these sea creatures in total came ashore? And what did they want?" Felipe asked as he knotted the sheet toga style, more to keep Jenny from stumbling off a cliff in distraction than out of modesty.

"Looks like there were five groups. Two sabotaged the quay. Another two went after our shanty village, while the last set—"

"Came after me," Jenny finished. "But why?"

"That's obvious," Felipe replied. "They were after you."

"Me? What for?"

"Maybe to prevent you from leaving," Felipe mused aloud. "They did, after all, destroy our means of departure."

"A good theory, but I think the better question to ask is who is behind the attack?" Teles remarked grimly as she marched. "Undines are basic and fairly mindless creatures. They don't act without orders."

"Who usually commands them?" Felipe asked.

Jenny and Teles exchanged a look, one that said they knew and really didn't like it. "Mermaids," they answered in unison.

And if mermaids were behind it, then not only did this involve Jenny he'd wager, but it probably had something to do with her mother.

Lucifer, you old devil, what scheme have you dropped me into now? Because he sure as fuck didn't believe in coincidences. If the mermaids were suddenly showing an interest in Jenny at the same time Lucifer was, then something was afoot.

And it didn't take an inner kitty's intrigue for him to suddenly want to know what.

Chapter Nine

A shiver shook Jenny as the cool, dead of night air kissed her skin, her fault for having forgotten to grab a shawl before rushing from her cave. A warm and heavy arm draped around her, drawing her close to a distinctly male body. Felipe's half-naked body. Felipe's magnificent body, which she swore had burned its imprint on her retina in the glimpse she got before he covered it up in some low, hip hugging jeans.

A proper young lady might have protested his familiarity, but her siren aunts raised her better than that. *After a man saves you from possible death and abduction, it seems stupid to shy away. Especially when he feels sooooo good.*

She snuggled closer. "I saw your cat. He's quite impressive." And beautiful with his striped fur, long tusked teeth and feline grace.

"He's also vain. So don't be shy with the compliments."

A giggle slipped out. "Does it hurt to change into your hellcat form?"

"Bah, a little discomfort is worth the result. When I'm in my feline shape, I'm stronger, faster, and my senses are more acute."

"So why bother ever shifting back?"

"I prefer my food cooked and my sex with a woman who can say more than meow."

Again, she couldn't help but laugh. "You are incorrigible."

"Rhymes with adorable."

And doable, but she kept that comparison to herself. "Thanks for coming to my rescue."

"My pleasure," he purred against her ear, a soft rumble that sent a shiver through her. The arm around her tightened, and a spurt of warmth that had nothing to do with body heat and lots to do with the sensual kind shot through her.

"Do you really think they were after me?"

"Yes. Someone doesn't want you leaving this island."

"And someone is asking for a serious ass kicking!" Thelxiope grumbled. Arriving behind them on the path, her prickly aunt removed Felipe's arm from around her and draped a cloak in its place. Shooting the hellcat a dark look, she grabbed Jenny by the forearm and tugged her ahead.

Felipe seemed more amused than offended by her actions, or so Jenny surmised by the smile lurking around the corner of his lips. With her grouchy aunt by her side and Teles leading the way, they entered the village where the captives were kept. And she did mean *were*.

The Undines had done quite a number on the place. Bodies littered the ground. Poor broken sailors who, bespelled by the sirens and without clear orders to guide them, were like lambs to the slaughter. Jenny gasped and covered her mouth at the carnage. Those poor lost souls. Literally.

Brought over from the mortal plane, it meant they had been alive. Not any longer. They'd died during the attack, and while their bodies littered the ground, their spirits remained, milling about uselessly, unsure of what to do.

"Well, this is a mess," Thelxiope complained with her hands planted on her hips.

"I've already put a call in to Charon," Raidne said as she exited a hut, rag in hand, scrubbing at the dark ichor staining her blade. "He's going to send a boat in the morning to pick the souls up."

Jenny went to speak, but Teles slapped a hand over her lips. "Shh. Not around the ghosts. We don't need another set of damned zombies on the island. Thank you very much. Why don't you go wait for us in Molpe's cave. It's closest. Bring your man with you."

My man? Hardly. Although it did have a nice ring.

Inclining her head in his direction, Jenny led Felipe down yet another tiki-torch-lined path to Molpe's hole in the ground. While Jenny and most of her aunts lived within the volcano, Molpe had taken over an underground cavern. An old lava tunnel apart from the others and close to the shanty village. It served her well in her task to watch over the captive males.

It also resembled a bordello, or so Thelxiope claimed every time they met there for dinner. Jenny wouldn't know, having never visited one.

"Your aunt has interesting taste," was Felipe's observation when they finished clambering down the carved steps into the huge cavern.

"If by interesting you mean a fetish for red, gold, and velvet, then yes." Jenny flopped onto an overstuffed couch with a deep seat and a ridiculous amount of pillows. Despite all the furniture around them, Felipe chose to sit alongside her.

"What was all that back there about zombies and ghosts?" he asked, seeming unperturbed by the fact his thigh pressed against hers.

She noticed it, but the plush seating wouldn't let her shift away without his notice, so she suffered—and enjoyed—the burning heat of him. "Another side effect of my voice."

"You're the reason why that escaped group of souls ended up useless to Lucifer?"

"Yeah, that was kind of my fault. It was foggy, and I was on watch, singing, when they came ashore. I didn't know they were there, or I would have stopped. Usually, mortals start screaming when they hear me sing, but apparently the damned are a little different. They ended up turning into zombies."

"Isn't that dangerous? I thought the undead were flesh-eating psychos?"

"Not these ones. I mean, they do eat flesh, dead or alive, but only when ordered. My aunts got permission from Lucifer to keep them for a while to use as a cleanup crew for bodies that wash ashore. It beats burning them."

"You've got a strange power, Jenny."

"I know," she said morosely, staring at her toes, which peeked out from the edge of the cloak. The polish on them was chipped. Imperfect. Just like her.

"Hey, don't look like that. I didn't mean it in a bad way." Calloused fingers tilted her chin up, and his golden eyes gazed into hers. "There's nothing wrong with being different. Look at me. The only cat shifter currently in Hell. I revel in my status instead of lamenting it."

"But it's easy for you. I mean, look at you. You're gorgeous and strong. Your kitty is freaking amazing. You've got lots to be proud of."

"And I think you're selling yourself short. In you, I see a beautiful, exotic woman with a power she's still learning to harness who just needs a little confidence in herself and the realization that unique is good. Different is sexy. And … irresistible." With that final whispered word, his lips founds hers, another kiss, this one a soft embrace, a sensual seduction.

Jenny melted. What defective mermaid wouldn't have? He said all the right things. He pressed all the right buttons. He made her feel *alive*.

She couldn't have said if she threw herself on his lap or he dragged her on to it. All she knew was she sat on him, squirming against his rigid shaft while their lips slid and tongues danced. Her hands roamed, touching the firm muscles of his arms, gliding along their solid expanse to caress the strong muscles of his shoulders before tangling in the silky softness of his hair. She wasn't alone in touching. His hands performed an exploration of their own.

One slid the length of her thigh while the other managed to cup a breast, a heavy breast with an aching peak. *Oh to feel his mouth on it.* She would have dragged his head to the spot in erotic demand if not for the cleared throat and titter of an audience.

"Would you like us to leave and come back in half an hour?" Molpe asked in clear amusement.

"Oh please, a randy young pair like that. They only need five, ten minutes tops," scoffed Raidne.

"Am I the only one disturbed by the fact our niece is making out with a stranger sent by Lucifer with a mission to steal her from us?" Thelxiope rudely added.

"Lighten up," Teles muttered, "you old, jealous hag."

"Hag! Old! I'll show you, beanpole."

Used to her aunts bickering, Jenny managed to tune them out but not enough to continue her make-out session with Felipe, enjoyable as she found it. With a sigh of regret, she relinquished his mouth, but when she went to move away to a spot on the couch, his arms tightened around her.

It seemed he didn't want her going anywhere. Rather than kick up a fuss, she nestled against him and watched her aunts face off.

"Do they do this often?" he murmured against her ear.

"Almost daily. Sometimes more than once. It's how they deal with the stress."

"Stress of what?"

"Knowing we're a dying breed," Raidne answered as she ignored her dueling siblings to seat herself across from them. "Once upon a time, sailors were plentiful, and we were fruitful. We had many daughters, and the island was full of life. Now…" She shook her head sadly. "We haven't seen a babe in over a century. It's why we so eagerly adopted our dear Jenny. Our visiting sailors have diminished in number, and those we do acquire don't seem to last as long as they used to. Nor are they able to father more sirens upon us. Something has changed."

"Something is coming," was Molpe's dire addition.

"You and your portents," scoffed Thelxiope, tossing her tousled hair over her shoulder and taking a regal seat in the club chair. Never mind the bruise darkening her cheek, or the split lip, she acted as if she hadn't just indulged in a catfight with Teles, who gripped a hank of hair in her hand and glared daggers at her sister.

"Laugh if you want, sister, but the signs have been getting clearer and the omens more obvious. Something deadly this way comes. From over the sea."

"There is nothing past the Darkling Sea," Teles said.

"How would you know?" Raidne asked. "No one has ever gone and returned to tell the tale."

"Perhaps what you sense is coming from the bottom of the sea." Felipe added his observation, and Jenny bit her lip.

The aunts all laughed.

"What? I don't see what's so funny."

"If there were something in the waves, we'd know. We know everything about these waters."

"But you didn't know the mermaids were planning an attack." His stark observation shut down the mirth.

"Don't you have a ball of yarn you should be playing with?"

"I prefer chasing down songbirds." His lips curled in mischief.

Thelxiope glared. "I don't like you."

"Does that mean you won't scratch me behind the ears?"

Jenny couldn't help a giggle.

Raidne snorted. "I wouldn't push her, cat. She's adept with a skinning knife."

"And we're getting off topic." Teles paced the edge of the living room space. "The cat is right about one thing though. We didn't have a clue the mermaids were capable of this kind of blatant treachery. I thought we had an understanding. What happened to the truce?"

"Truce?"

Molpe explained it to Felipe. "Sirens and mermaids need males, preferably human ones, to procreate. There was a time when we used to fight over them and, in the process, wasted a lot of potential seamen."

A snicker escaped Raidne. "And semen."

"Anyhow, we came to an agreement. A boundary of sorts. Ships that sailed into or wrecked in a certain area were ours to keep, those outside of it, theirs. And it's been that way for centuries," Molpe said, and then in a more ominous undertone, "Until now."

"I still can't believe they dared send their mutant progeny to attack."

Felipe held up a hand. "Progeny? Hold on a second. I thought you said mermaids had only girls."

"If they mate with humans. But sometimes the mermaids outnumber the males, and needs must be met. In their fish form, there are other ways of getting pregnant. The results of that are the Undines. Male warriors. Drones in a sense really with no true sense of self. Born and bred purely for protection of the schools."

"And now being used to break the peace," Raidne added.

"This means war!" Thelxiope declared.

"Oh take a pill. We aren't going to war with the mermaids, but they will have to answer for their attack."

"Could it be Jenny's mother trying to take her back?" Felipe asked.

The sirens exchanged looks, and Jenny frowned. "Doubtful," was Raidne's careful reply.

"Why doubtful? She dumped me here. Maybe she changed her mind." Which still didn't make sense. While Jenny had never seen mermaids in these waters, it didn't mean her mother couldn't have swam to the shores and called for her or given her conch a call.

"Well…" Molpe stretched the word.

"Oh just tell her. It's about time she knew," Teles said.

"Are you sure?" Raidne asked.

"Sure of what?" Peering at their faces, Jenny could admit complete confusion.

"Oh for Neptune's sake. Just spit it out. It wasn't your mother that dumped you here," Thelxiope barked.

"I don't understand."

"Your mother doesn't know where you are."

"You mean she didn't abandon me?" Jenny's heart stuttered.

"You'd better tell her all of it," Molpe muttered, "before she finds out."

A heavy sigh left Teles. "Don't freak out, but you were left here, without your mother's knowledge, to save your life. It seems your mother plotted to kill you. Someone who didn't approve of her plan found out and rescued you and brought you to our shores knowing we'd take you in and protect you."

Jenny blinked. Long. Slow. Trying to digest it, but stumbling mentally. "She wanted me dead?"

"Very. She had an accident all planned out so the other mermaids wouldn't find out. But one of the sea creatures she tried to drag into her plan tattled on her, and before she could implement her dastardly scenario, you were rescued."

"And you've known all this time."

It didn't take the four sets of eyes refusing to meet hers to get an answer.

"But why did she want me dead?"

"Why doesn't matter. What does matter is the fact we love you, as you are, and have always thought of you as a daughter, so who cares what one warped mermaid thinks?"

But Jenny did care, even if she shouldn't. *My own mother hated me enough to want me dead.* No wonder her aunts kept the truth from her. Felipe's arms tightened around her and whispered, "Listen to your aunts. And remember what I said. You are special."

So special her mother couldn't wait to try to kill her again once she found her. "You think she's the one behind the attack, don't you? Is she also the one keeping me prisoner on this island? Has she made a deal with the Styx monsters to keep me prisoner?"

Four sets of eyes found much of interest in the ceiling of the room.

"What? You're also responsible for that?"

"We did it for your own good," Molpe explained. "Since we feared an assassination attempt, we made a deal with the Styx monsters to keep you on the isle and to prevent the mermaids from approaching and discovering your presence."

"You really think she would have come after me?" Jenny's heart ached. Even with the tight hug of Felipe's arms and the sadness in her aunts' eyes showing the depth of their caring, she couldn't quite shrug it off. "This is unbelievable."

"I wonder how she found out you were here," mused Raidne aloud. "Someone must have tattled."

"Whoever it is, they'll be dealt with," Thelxiope grimly announced.

"Indeed they shall, but in the meantime, we need to keep our darling Jenny safe."

"I think I can provide aid there," Felipe said, finally adding his voice to the discussion. "Let me take her to meet Lucifer. Once she's in the inner ring under the Dark Lord's protection, none will dare mess with her."

"Except you don't know what he wants her for."

"I can assure you, whatever his reason, he wants her alive, though," was Felipe's retort.

"True." Teles took on a pensive look. "The Undines wouldn't be able to reach her there. Too far from the shores of the sea."

"Hold on a second." Jenny waved her hand to draw attention. "I never said I wanted to go. I'm not a coward to run away. This is my mother you believe who is attacking the isle, which makes this my problem. My fight. I should be staying to deal with it."

"Have we taught you nothing?" Molpe chided. "Altruism is for heroes and those with a death wish. We are sirens."

"Not all of us," Jenny muttered.

"Adopted counts," Molpe said sternly. "And besides, we are still your guardians. If we say you're going, then you will go."

Determined to face her past, Jenny stood and glared. "I am a grown woman, and I say no. This is my life, which means I get to choose what happens to me."

Or not.

Chapter Ten

Hearing Jenny's life story, and, worse, seeing, even feeling, the emotions coursing through her at the news of her mother's perfidy, struck at Felipe's heart.

He couldn't blame her for wanting to remain and confront the mermaid determined to mistreat her. So it was with more than a little shock that he watched as her grumpy aunt conked her on the head with the butt of the dagger she kept at her waist. Poor Jenny, practically mid sentence, her eyes rolled up in her head, and only his quick reflexes managed to catch her before she hit the floor.

"What the fuck was that for?" he yelled, doing his best to quell his snarling inner feline.

Thelxiope shrugged. "She was being stubborn, and I wasn't in the mood to waste time arguing."

That was her reasoning? "You hit her!"

"It was just a little tap, and she'll heal quick enough."

"But why?" Felipe asked, dividing his attention between the limp, vulnerable woman in his arms and the one his cat wanted to skin alive.

"Are you deaf? I wasn't in the mood to waste another moment. We need to get her off this island."

"You could have spent a few more minutes trying to convince her."

"You know, I much prefer a man who does as he's told instead of disagreeing with me," grumbled Thelxiope.

"Then you've been missing out," snarled Felipe. "Might as well invest in some vibrators if all you want is a well-behaved cock."

Raidne stifled a giggle. Thelxiope glowered, and her dagger lifted in a menacing fashion.

"I think we all need to calm down," Molpe said in an attempt to mediate.

Hackles raised and thoroughly irritated—less by the conversation and more by the injury done to Jenny—Felipe wasn't in the mood to back down. "I'll calm the fuck down when this psycho stops acting like such a bitch."

"Thelxy, why don't you just apologize? Poor Felipe here isn't used to your ways."

"You're taking his side? Well, I never," huffed Thelxiope. "And I am not apologizing to this animal."

"Then why don't you go work on our defenses in case the Undines come back? We'll deal with our feline visitor and Jenny."

With a sniff of disdain, the regal and irritable siren spun on her heel and stalked off, leaving Felipe alone with the other three. "What did you mean by deal with?" he asked. "Going to conk me over the head too?"

"Of course not. Anyone can tell your skull is too thick for that to work." Raidne grinned. "You can stop looking like such a sour puss. While Thelxy's methods are brash, you can't deny they're effective. What do you say we get you and Jenny out of here before she wakes and the mermaids realize their attack failed?"

"And how do you propose to do that? My boat was sunk, and Charon will take at least a day or more to get a new boat out here."

Raidne laughed. "Oh please. Wait for one of those archaic pole barges? Silly kitty. We've had ships sailing into our waters from the interdimensional rip for centuries. Do you truly think we've let all of them crash on the rocks?"

Apparently, they hadn't. It seemed sirens enjoyed collecting more than just treasures and seamen.

Felipe gaped at the two-hundred-plus-foot white yacht bobbing in yet another underground cavern, this one filled with water and ships of various sizes and eras. A wooden schooner with actual masts and rolled sails. A rugged-looking tug. A fishing vessel still decorated with a suspended net and mounted harpoon.

"This is incredible," he complimented, impressed despite himself.

"Yes. Yes it is," Teles agreed. "But the better question is, can you pilot one of these things?"

The masculine part of him urged him to lie and say yes. However, truth—an annoying habit Lucifer abhorred—wouldn't let him. "No. If this were a car or motorcycle, we'd be okay. But when it comes to water, my skills are for fishing, not sailing."

"No problem. I'll drive." Molpe hitched her skirts as she clambered the ladder bolted to the side of the towering white yacht, aptly named *Wave Singer*.

"Here's a bag of Jenny's things." Raidne handed him a large knapsack. "I packed one while you were washing off the Undine goo."

A shower he'd much needed and appreciated. "Thanks. What are you and the others going to do while I bring Jenny to the inner ring?"

"Batten down the hatches. Prepare our defenses and then call in some favors. Those fish-tailed bitches won't be getting away with this attack. Before we're done, the sea will run red with their blood. And all will remember why you never fuck with a siren—unless you're a tall, handsome seaman. Those we screw with pleasure." Raidne winked, and Felipe shook his head.

The sirens might seem ladylike on the outside. However, like all things residing on the Hellish plane, they were bloodthirsty, vengeful creatures. *My kind of gals.*

Tossing the knapsack overhand, he heard it land on deck with a thump. Then, with Jenny slung over his shoulder, Felipe clambered the ladder onto the giant yacht. In moments, they cast off, the rocking of the waves barely noticeable on deck. Not that he stayed above for long. He needed to get Jenny to safety.

Despite the sirens' reassurances that the Styx monsters would now let her pass, their edict to keep her island-bound lifted, he didn't trust them. Better to have her out of sight than accidentally snatched from the deck by some long-tentacled creature.

Below deck proved as luxurious as above with a living area covered in wall-to-wall cream carpeting and a curved sofa made of buttery-soft tan leather. He opted to place her on that couch rather than in one of the two bedrooms, figuring

close at hand was better than the extra comfort—
and temptation—of a bed.

Laying her out, he couldn't help but brush
her silky green hair, the backs of his knuckles
stroking the smooth skin of her cheek.

He barely knew the girl, yet something
about her called to him. Struck a chord. He didn't
understand what it was, or why, but, as a wild
creature of Hell, and a man who lived by trusting
his instincts, he didn't fight it. If his gut said to
protect her, he would. If his cat said to keep her
close, he'd listen. And if his heart said she was the
one…

Meowr! Where did that stray thought
come from? The one? As if! Felipe wasn't the type
to settle down. He was a tomcat, a lover of many,
not the boyfriend of one. It was just the
excitement of the moment making him think that
way. Perhaps even a touch of magic? No way was
he changing his ways. No matter how cute and
appealing Jenny was.

Still, reminding himself of that fact didn't
stop him from placing a soft kiss on her lips or
drawing an afghan he found in the closet over
her.

With her safely tucked away, he returned
above deck to act as lookout. And to get more
answers.

He joined Molpe, who handled the
steering of the boat with ease.

"I'm surprised to see you. I thought you'd
be keeping our girl company."

"I'd rather be close by in case of trouble."

"Probably a wise decision, but I'll bet not
your only reason for joining me."

"Is my curiosity that obvious?"

"Yes, as is your interest in my niece."

Purely professional and sexual interest, nothing more, no matter what his inner kitty seemed to think. "She's intriguing."

"Is that all?" Molpe asked, not even bothering to hide the lilting amusement in her voice.

"And sexy."

"About time someone noticed."

As if other men hadn't noted Jenny's beauty. Then again, on second thought, he was kind of glad they hadn't. He quite enjoyed her somewhat innocent responses to his advances. *Pink blushes and soft kisses purely for me.*

Despite his lack of reply, Molpe continued to speak. "Although, I'll wager she'll get plenty of attention in Hell's capital. I'm sure you won't be the only male immune to her special brand of magic. Why in no time at all, she'll probably have a bevy of suitors, and…" Molpe cast him a sly smirk. "Lovers."

What? Like Hell. He couldn't help the low growl that spilled from his lips. *Mine.* The possessive emotion didn't just come from the cat. He couldn't help but feel it too. The idea of Jenny sharing her smiles, her lips, her body—

No! I won't share. Jealousy for something other than his adopted witch mother or food took him by surprise. Since when did he care what a woman did once they parted ways? He had no interest in settling down. Tomcats fucked. Tomcats roamed. Tomcats did not want to rip to shreds anyone who thought to make advances on a mermaid who wasn't a mermaid.

Until now.

Uh-oh. Felipe didn't like what this meant. Good thing this yacht could move because the quicker he got rid of his green-haired temptress, the better. Before he did something stupid. Something permanent. Something—ugh—domestic.

Chapter Eleven

Jenny awoke to a dull throb in her head. *Oh no, don't tell me I got drunk on seaweed wine again. What happened to my vow the last time to never touch a drop again?*

Except, now that she thought on it, she'd not drank. On the contrary, the last thing she recalled was arguing with her aunts. Before she could muddle through her dizzy thoughts, which weren't aided by the rocking room, Felipe's anxious expression appear in front of hers.

"What happened?" she asked.

"We're on a yacht bound for Hell."

"A yacht? But how?"

"Thelxiope."

And that one word said it all.

With her fingers, she pressed the bump on her noggin and growled, "Aunt Thelxy!" She should have known right away who to blame. It wouldn't be the first time her aunt solved a problem in this fashion.

But this was the first time Jenny had regained consciousness to find herself on a boat sailing to who knew where. She recognized the rocking motion and subtle purr of an engine.

Why those conniving witches. They'd kidnapped her. Kind of. Maybe pirated was more accurate given the situation.

Clambering to her feet, she noted someone had bathed and dressed her during her forced siesta. She now wore a slim-fitting sweater, canvas slacks but no shoes—or a bra or underwear. *Must have been Aunt Raidne.* She thought undergarments were a waste of fabric unless worn for seduction.

"Where are you going?" Felipe asked.

"To talk with my aunt."

"Shouldn't you rest a while longer. She hit you pretty hard."

"I'll be fine," she grumbled, especially once the three pain killers she found in the cabinet and dry swallowed kicked in.

The ache in her head abated, leaving her more alert. In need of answers, and maybe a little venting, Jenny made her way to the upper deck, the brisk, damp breeze whipping her greenish strands around her face as whoever piloted cut through the agitated waves. Above deck, the roll of the ship was more noticeable, and Jenny adopted a loose-legged saunter as she made her way to the captain's cockpit. What a surprise. Aunt Molpe steered the boat and tossed her a saucy grin.

"Ahoy there, little mate. Have a nice nap?"

"Concussions aren't restful."

"But they can be useful when dealing with stubborn girls."

"It's not stubborn to have an opinion."

"It is when it's the wrong one."

"I can't believe you went along with this," Jenny grumbled. "You know I didn't want to leave."

"Yes, but in this instance, Thelxy was right. You had to go. If the mermaids and their servants were to come after us in full force, we'd never be able to protect you. Then where would you be?"

"So instead of seeing me possibly fed to the fish, you left your sisters undermanned by removing not only me but yourself from the defense of the isle."

A shrug. "More like saved them. With you gone, the chance of attack drops drastically is our theory, and they won't be undermanned for long. We've got our resources, and they're being called in."

"Then why not let me stay?"

Molpe's usually cheerful mien sobered. "Because staying means they win. Someone, or many someones, don't want you to go see Lucifer."

"So you just had to do the opposite." Jenny rolled her eyes.

"Of course we did," was Molpe's unapologetic reply. "That and we couldn't let the kitty return empty-handed, not when it was obvious you'd both taken such a shine to each other."

"Did not."

"Oh please, we're not blind or dead. We know lust when we see it. About time, if you ask me, that you found someone who gets your motor running."

"Just because he's attractive isn't a reason for me to go off with him." Or screw him. Okay, maybe having sex with him would be good for her, but still. They were talking about a life-altering event. Leaving home, especially now, seemed, well, crazy. Dangerous. Adventurous. And fun. Sigh. She hated it when her aunts were right.

Aunt Molpe seemed to have taken quite a shine to the hellcat. "Our new friend, Felipe, is not just attractive. He's brave. Intelligent. And, in case you haven't noticed, he can listen to you without jumping off a cliff."

True. Arguing any further was pointless. Like it or not, ready or not, Jenny was getting shoved out of the nest for the unknown. Despite herself, Jenny couldn't deny excitement at finally getting a chance to leave the isle. Discovery awaited. New shores. New people. A new life…

"So we're heading to Hell?"

"Indeed we are. We've been following the coastline for the outer ring for the past hour."

"And the Styx monsters are behaving?"

"Of course they are. They only prevented you from leaving before at our behest."

"Well, that's good to know because, otherwise, I might be kind of worried about *that.*" Just as Jenny pointed to a shadowy shape paralleling the vessel underwater, the boat lurched.

The steering column jolted, and Molpe clung to it, straining to keep it straight. She righted it, but how long they would stay that way would depend on the humps breaking the surface of the water, the undulating shapes racing alongside them, and without much care for the hapless vessel they rocked.

"What are they doing?" Jenny asked. A valid question given a huge, barnacle-covered head rose from the frothy waters and peered at them through a gigantic lidless eye. Considering it was almost as big as she was, she thought she had a right to shiver.

Another sign that signified they might be in trouble, carefree Molpe frowned. "I'm not sure what they're up to. This isn't behavior I'm used to seeing from them, but, if I were to guess, given their numbers and the fact the predators are ignoring possible meals and they're all going in the same direction, I'd say they're fleeing."

The observation made Jenny's eyes widen. "Fleeing? What the heck makes a giant sea serpent swim away?"

"That's what I'd like to know, 'cause for once it isn't me," Felipe announced as he entered the now much smaller cockpit, his large masculine presence overwhelming the space. And he would steal all the oxygen too by dropping a chaste—but toe-curling—kiss on her lips. "Hello again, beautiful. Nice to see you've recovered from your impromptu nap."

"Um, hi." More speech wasn't happening, not until the world stopped tilting. Not likely to happen soon, given the thumps and bumps hammering the yacht from both sides as the water around them erupted with the frantic jump and dive of fish, the undulation of serpents, and the occasional jagged fin.

"What in Neptune's beard is going on?" Molpe muttered under her breath as she struggled to keep the yacht from capsizing in a suddenly very busy part of the Styx.

Jenny craned to peer out the window, the orange light of dawn, and Hell's natural ambiance, providing a glow to see by. "Um, Aunt, is it me, or are those storm clouds behind us?"

"A storm, at this time of the year?" Molpe gestured for her to grab the controls and went out on deck to take a peek.

She returned quickly with ashen cheeks and practically hip checked Jenny out of the way. "Hold on, children. We need to get out of here."

"Why? What's wrong?"

"That's not a natural storm."

"Is it weather witches fucking around?" Felipe asked.

"I wish. That we could have handled. But witches don't have the power to cause what I saw. A cyclone is brewing behind us. We need to try and outrun it and make it to shore before it catches us."

"A cyclone, here on the river?" Jenny frowned. "I thought those only happened at sea."

"They do, which means this one isn't natural." Grim-faced, Molpe pushed the throttle as far as it would go, the burst of speed causing them all to stagger before catching their balance, a balance that found Jenny leaning against a rock-hard body.

"You said you know how to swim?" Felipe asked, his warm breath right by her ear.

"Of course. I just can't breathe underwater."

"Good."

"Why do you ask?"

However, she didn't need to hear his reply to realize they weren't going to make it to shore before the fast-moving cyclone hit them. The waves grew choppier and choppier, rocking the boat in a sickening fashion from side to side. Molpe did her best to steer, but the strain showed on her face in the tense line of her lips and the rarely seen creases of stress around her eyes and forehead.

"We're not going to hit the beach before the storm hits us," she muttered. "Grab a life vest and buckle in, children. Looks like we're going for a dip."

As they scrambled to attire themselves in the bright orange safety devices that the sirens kept on board, Jenny couldn't help but notice Felipe's ashen face.

"Are you scared?"

Most men would have probably lied, or so her aunts' lessons had taught her, but Felipe was a never-ending surprise. "I hate water," was his grudging admission. "Or at least the whole submerging myself in it part. It's not natural."

"And yet you shower."

"Quickly, and I prefer to think of that more like rain which I can easily step out of. Swimming, though, means sinking into a whole bunch of it at once, and I hate it."

"Don't be such a pussy," Molpe taunted.

Felipe's lips twisted into a wry smile. "But I am a pussy, and my pussy doesn't like to get wet!"

Jenny couldn't have said what prompted her to say it, but the look on his face was worth it. "Funny you should say that because, since I met you, my pussy's never been wetter. And might I add, I quite enjoy it."

Forget a reply. She had only a moment to enjoy his dropped jaw before the storm hit. The boat tilted and tilted some more. But this time, it's didn't bob back upright. It capsized in the water, sending them tumbling into the warm waters of the Styx, where up and down, surface and bottom got mixed around.

Realizing that fighting the waves and currents would tax her strength more than it was worth, Jenny relaxed. Besides, she wore a life jacket. It knew better than her how to find the surface. She floated underwater, arms and legs spread a la starfish, letting the river take her where it would. Hopefully to shore where most waves tended to land.

A hard knock to her arm had her opening her eyes, and despite the cloudy murk, she caught the vague glimpse of flesh. Waving hands. Wide white panicked eyes.

Felipe!

She managed to clasp her fingers around his, forcing him to face her underwater, bringing them close, trying to instill some of her calm to the agitated cat. But in his angst, he'd used up much of his air. His eyes bulged, and she could see the strain as he fought not to breathe in the deadly water.

Drawing him near, she pressed her mouth to his, sealed them together, and blew. It took him but a moment to grasp what she did. He sucked in, and while it didn't ease the tension she felt trembling through his frame, it did stem some of his panic.

A strong surge propelled them, and for a moment, their heads broke the surface. She drew in a deep breath and smiled approvingly at Felipe as he took in one of his own. Their oxygenated reprieve lasted but a moment before another wave rolled over them, drawing them under again. But at least now he wasn't freaking out and using up his oxygen. Fingers and eyes locked, they held their breath, blowing out little bubbles, doing their best to remain alive until they had a chance to suck in a lungful.

How long they drifted, flotsam caught in a wild, unnatural storm, she couldn't tell. Several more times, she had to give Felipe air, the press of their lips an intimate act which didn't arouse—

how could it given the circumstances?—but yet, it still forged a bond between them. A bond of life over death. A bond of trust. Odd how the danger they were in, more than any words, could create such a solid thread.

When her feet first dragged along the pebbled bottom, she wondered if she imagined it. It seemed they'd bobbed along in weightless space for an eternity. A wave drew them up, not long enough for her to truly note anything, but when it dropped, again she hit a solid surface, and Felipe noted it as well. The fingers laced with hers tightened, and he pushed himself to stand, only to get knocked down by the next swell. However, as the water grew shallow, he managed to keep to his feet, even steady her on her own.

Bedraggled, exhausted, and more shriveled than any raisin left in the sun, they made it to shore and collapsed. Breathing heavy, enjoying the brimstone-laced air, the hard surface, and the lack of rocking, Jenny and Felipe took a moment to appreciate having survived.

Or at least she did. The cat, however, complained. "Ugh. That is the last time I ever go sailing."

For some reason, Jenny found that immensely funny. She commenced laughing, almost hysterically, until he muffled her with a kiss—a kiss that stole breath instead of giving it.

Chapter Twelve

Soggy. Wrinkled. Exhausted, with possibly a fish or two caught in his pants.

Despite the unromantic situation, Felipe had no problem finding the good in the moment. For one, he was alive. Two, he'd not used up any of his lives. And three, he kissed the most amazing woman he'd ever met.

Without her, he would have drowned. He wasn't too macho to admit it. When he hit the water, despite the lifejacket—and his extra lives— he freaked. As a result of his panic, he used up his oxygen too fast, a problem compounded when he couldn't find the surface. Then, as if things weren't bad enough, flotation device or not, he felt himself sinking. With lungs straining, his kitty practically catatonic, and about to breathe in water, Jenny took him in hand. She saved him.

She not only breathed life into him, she calmed him and kept hold of him even during the roughest of tumbles through vicious waves and currents. With single-mindedness and courage, she forced him to focus on her, showed him he could trust her with his life.

To one such as him, used to roaming alone and giving his loyalty to no one but the witch who raised him, this was huge. It went beyond huge; it was life altering. Mind-boggling. Freaky.

Washing ashore was euphoric. Solid ground never felt more wonderful. And hearing her laugh? The most sensual sound he'd ever heard.

He didn't kiss her to shut her up or because she mocked his heartfelt words. *No way am I sailing again!* He kissed her because he wanted to keep the connection between them. He needed to make sure the bond they'd forged while flotsam in the wild storm remained intact. And he selfishly wanted to get her naked to fuck.

Nothing like facing mortality—or at least one of his lives at any rate—to bring out the horncat in him.

He rolled atop her, their lips joined and his tongue questing. She met him, kiss for kiss, her breathing erratic, her need just as frantic. While he'd lost his boots during their swim, the life vest remained, making their attempt to grope frustrating.

With a growl he leapt to his feet and, with clumsy, pruned fingers, attempted to unbuckle the blasted thing.

She, of course, giggled, and he glared at her, not too angrily. She truly was picture perfect lying sprawled on her back on the sandy shore, her wet hair spread around her in a halo, her lips curved in mirth.

"This isn't funny."

"Lighten up, kitty. We're alive. If we can survive a cyclone, I'm pretty sure you can handle a simple fluorescent vest."

Yes he could. He popped a claw and sliced through the damned straps until he could peel the hated thing from his body. Then, as she still laughed, he took care of hers. Tossing it to the side, he dragged her onto his lap.

"Where were we?" he murmured, a hairsbreadth from her lips.

"I don't know where you were," interrupted an amused voice, "but I can tell you where you are, and it's not a motel. Although, if you don't mind an audience, and possibly seeing your sex tape on Helltube later on, then, by all means, carry on."

Felipe blamed the water in his ears—and seasick cat—for not noting the stranger who'd snuck up on them. With a curse—that was mild compared to what Jenny was capable of—he sprang to his feet to face the newcomer.

Standing almost eye-to-eye with him was a warrior woman. Tanned, lean, muscled, with her hair tightly braided and wound atop her head, the female eyed him with a smirk as she leaned against her spear. "Let me know when you're done ogling."

Jenny shouldered her way in front of him and, despite her shorter stature, seemed determined to cover his body with her own. "Stand back."

The barbarian winced at the sound of Jenny's voice but didn't cower. "Did the sea render you hoarse?"

"No. I always speak like this. And this is nothing. If I don't get answers, I'll start to sing."

Grimacing, the woman didn't start bleeding from any orifices, which Felipe took as a good sign given what he knew of Jenny's power.

"And I thought I had a rough voice. Hope you don't talk a lot."

"Who are you? And where are we?" Jenny asked.

"Shouldn't I be asking the questions?"

Felipe jumped in before Jenny sang and killed the warrior woman before they got answers. "Listen, we're just looking for some answers, not trouble." He paired his soothing words with a smile. It worked. The stranger softened, but Jenny stiffened and shot him an annoyed glance.

"I'm Valasca. Warrior and hunter for the Amazon tribe who lives upon the cliffs."

Great. From one matriarchal situation to another. Was Felipe cursed to deal with women who thought men were only good for one thing? *And yet, ironically, before I began my voyage, wasn't fucking my only concern?*

Funny how seeing and encountering women who lived with that belief was causing him to re-evaluate his own perceptions on life and his role for the future. *Perhaps it's time I worried less about screwing and more about what true skills I have to offer.*

Ugh. Please don't say I'm growing up finally.

"How did you find us?"

"I was scouting our beach for debris. You never know what, or who, you'll find."

"Have you seen another person wash ashore?" Jenny asked. "A woman with blonde hair, kind of short and chubby. We were sailing with my aunt when the storm caught us."

The Amazon shook her head. "Sorry. You're the only living thing to wash up on the shores that didn't have fins."

Seeing Jenny shiver, Felipe resumed his role of protector. "Do you have some shelter we can borrow? Dry clothes, too, and food? I've got no coin to currently pay you with, but if you send a message to Lord Lucifer, he will pay any and all expenses we incur outfitting ourselves that we might continue our journey."

"I've got all that. But might I ask, why journey when you can use a portal?"

"You have one?"

"Of course," she scoffed. "We're barbarians, not cavewomen. We have one that leads to the third ring."

"Why the third?" he asked. Most chose the fourth or fifth ring, which was where most of the shops and trade goods were found.

"Best demonic horseflesh in the nine circles." She stated this as if it were the most obvious thing in Hades.

"Can you take us to it?"

"After we get changed," Jenny interrupted. "I am not going to meet Lucifer in rags and stinking of the river."

Felipe opened his mouth to retort that, given the events, speed was of essence but took note of her cute, if bedraggled, state. He also noted the lines of exhaustion. When meeting the Lord of the Pit, it was best to have all your wits about you. It wouldn't kill them—he hoped—to delay by one day, or at least a night to allow her time to rest and recoup her strength.

"How safe is your village?"

He accepted Valasca's belly laugh as answer.

With his hand laced around one of Jenny's, he followed the warrior woman along a path that wound steeply, following the craggy cliff face.

Jenny was silent at his side, and he could guess the reason. "I'm sure your aunt is fine."

Troubled blue eyes met his. "Probably. It would take more than a capsized boat to kill my aunt Molpe. What's more worrisome is how it happened in the first place. Cyclones don't happen on the Styx. Heck, according to my lessons, they're rare even at sea. The kind of power needed to create that kind of storm…" Jenny gnawed her lip. "This wasn't mermaids."

"And you've no idea who else has that kind of power?"

She shook her head.

"From what I know, Gaia has caused more than her fair share of super storms on the mortal plane."

"You're speaking of Mother Earth? I learned about her in history class. She even visited my aunts once when I was young. And yes, she's capable, on the mortal plane where her magic is strong. But here in Hell, over the Styx, which is kind of a no-woman's land? It was my understanding that no one could control it like that."

After that, they traveled again in silence, each lost in their thoughts, Jenny fretting about who could possibly want her dead and where her aunt ended up. Or so he guessed. He, on the other hand, wondered how he would explain to his boss the delay and the fact that some unknown power was messing around in his domain.

Lucifer didn't take well to challenges. Actually, that wasn't quite accurate. His boss always faced threats to his reign head-on—usually by tossing legions of minions at it. It usually didn't bode well for the minions.

Which led him to think about the sexy lady who was his mission. Yes, speed was of essence, yet he couldn't deny Jenny's simple request to replenish themselves, not when it would probably align with his plan to seduce her. He wondered if they could manage any privacy in the village. A bed wouldn't hurt either. Then again, he'd had many a pleasant encounter in an alley against a wall. But for some reason, he wanted something a little more private and comfortable for his first time with Jenny.

The so-called Amazon village proved a lot more sophisticated than he would have imagined. Fortress-like and ringed with a wall of stone, the tops of which were guarded by more women sporting bows, the heavy portcullis clanged loudly behind them.

Felipe arched a brow at the heavy defense. "Expecting an attack?"

Shooting him a glance over her shoulder, Valasca grinned. "Always. Only the unprepared get taken by surprise."

Well, duh. He didn't say it aloud though, not with the dozens of flinty stares aimed his way. Of more concern than the ones that promised bodily harm were those appraising him much as he would horseflesh. Those women eyed him up and down, spending more time than he liked on his midsection. He didn't protest when Jenny, with tight lips, laced her fingers in his, for comfort or jealous claim, he didn't care. He'd hide behind her skirts if it kept him safe from these man-eaters.

And I thought the nymphs were dangerous. At lease they left their men alive, if exhausted. These Amazons though … he'd heard rumors.

"Are there no men here?" Jenny asked. An innocuous question, yet several shrieks were uttered, moans of pain, and a plump seagull hit the ground with a thud at her feet.

"What just happened?" Valasca demanded.

Chagrined, Jenny hunched in on herself as her power inadvertently manifested. Squeezing her fingers in invisible support, Felipe explained. "Jenny's voice can have unfortunate side effects."

"It didn't on me."

"Those who are tone-deaf seem to fare best against it, but others…" He gestured at the glares, nose bleeds, and women holding hands to their heads. "I guess this answers our question as to how widespread the problem is."

"I think it best you keep quiet until you speak with our elder," Valasca declared.

"What happened to food and shelter?"

"You'll get it. After you meet with Thora. It's protocol that all visitors be presented to her before given accommodations within our walls."

Less presented and more like examined. Valasca led them into a large room, a dining hall he'd wager given the table and benches set in a U shape, which at its peak boasted a table on the dais. And seated at the table in a chair whose back arched higher than the others was an old woman. Old in presence, not features.

Felipe hadn't quite yet figured out what the Amazons were. Gossip held they were related to the Valkyries, blessed by the ancient Viking gods and given special status when they died. Not entirely human, their smell wasn't quite right and, yet, not demon. What did that leave?

A mystery that he'd delve into if he ever found the time. Right now wasn't the moment.

"Elder, I found these two washed upon the shores. This is Felipe, one of Lucifer's minions and Jenny, from Siren Isle, his companion."

Sharp green eyes perused them from a face tanned by the outdoors. "A hellcat. It's been a while since I've seen one of your kind."

Felipe couldn't help the surprise in his tone. "You know what I am?"

The elder waved a hand. "Of course. Anyone with eyes in their head could. Your coloring, and bearing, not to mention your eyes, give it away. But your friend, on the other hand…" The woman leaned forward and subjected Jenny to a more intense stare. "She is different. New. What are you, child?"

Jenny peered at him, lips clamped, fearful of speaking he'd wager.

"Don't look to him for approval. I'm speaking to you."

"Jenny's afraid to—"

"Silence, cat. I was speaking to the girl." The elder waved her hand at him.

His kitty wanted to bat at it. How dare she order him to shut up! He would have said something to that effect; however, to Felipe's annoyance, he found his lips wouldn't move. His eyes narrowed, and the elder smirked at him.

Magic.

Jenny must have caught a hint because she drew her shoulders back. "Leave him alone. He's just trying to protect you from my voice."

To the elder's credit, she didn't grimace, but the guards near her throne didn't fare as well.

One dropped her spear to grab at her nose, which gushed blood, while another keeled right over with a clatter.

Valasca snorted. "Weaklings."

The elder appeared taken aback. "So the rumors are true. You've a deadly siren's voice."

Jenny shook her head.

"Not deadly?"

She shook again.

"Not a siren?"

A nod was followed by Jenny shrugging.

"Do you know what you are?"

When Jenny hesitated, the elder waved at her guards to leave. "We're alone now. You may speak freely."

"I'm half mermaid, ma'am."

"The other half being?"

"Unknown. My siren aunts think I might have some of their blood in there, though, given my power."

"How far reaching is your gift?"

"Far enough. And it's not just people who are affected."

"Fascinating," the elder mused aloud as she leaned back in her seat.

"Not really."

"You don't enjoy being able to conquer with just your voice?"

"I'd rather be able to hold a conversation with people without them throwing themselves off a cliff," was Jenny's dry reply. "It makes for short friendships."

Thora snorted. "What if I could help you with that?"

"Why would you? And how?"

"The how is easy. I have an amulet, a spelled one, which the sirens use when they come ashore to protect those listening from their voice. We trade with them every so often and found ear plugs to be inefficient with the more weak-minded."

"You think it would work with me?"

"We can certainly give it a try."

"But why? Why would you give it to me?"

"Why not? I sense things about you, child. Your fate is somehow interwoven into that of the upcoming skirmish."

What skirmish? Felipe wanted to ask; however, he still couldn't move, only listen.

"What do you know of my fate and what is coming?" Jenny queried. "Why have I suddenly become so important? Only a few days ago, I was a nobody. Just a defective mermaid and siren, torturing those unfortunate enough to hear my song. Now I've got things trying to kill me, storms trying to drown me, Lucifer taking an interest, and you wanting to help. You'll forgive me if I don't understand why this is all happening."

"And we might never know. The planes move in mysterious ways. There are forces at work whose goal none can guess. We can only do our best to survive." Thora removed a gold chain from around her neck. From it dangled a pearl-like jewel, its color shifting as it spun on the end. "Try this on."

"And if I don't want your gift?"

The elder laughed and shrugged. "Then don't take it. I'm not going to force you. Nor do I want payment. But I want a promise."

And here came the catch.

Jenny's eyes narrowed in suspicion. "What kind of promise?"

"If there is to be a battle, you will call upon us. My warriors tire of the minor fights and long for the days gone by when epic wars were fought. We missed out on the last rebellion in Hell due to our allowing ourselves to fall out of the loop. We don't want to be forgotten again."

Lips pursed and brow knit, Jenny replied. "That's it? You just want me to tell you when and where to fight?"

Thora nodded, and Valasca couldn't stop herself either it seemed from her own vigorous agreement.

"Done." The promise practically echoed, as if someone, or something, took note. Felipe couldn't help but think the choice made in this room had narrowed the branches of the future. A future Jenny would play a part in.

As Thora twitched the amulet, gesturing for Jenny to take it, the spell holding Felipe let go, but he wisely held his tongue. No need to irritate the elder, not when it seemed she wished them no harm.

"Valasca will show you to your quarters and have refreshments brought to you along with fresh garments. Rest, and in the morn, we will send you through our portal."

With a wave of her hand, Thora dismissed them. Following Valasca's lead, they exited the grand chamber back into the large courtyard. However, before they'd made it halfway across, Felipe heard some ominous words that made him wonder just how much more trouble his simple mission to fetch Jenny would face.

Chapter Thirteen

Lucifer drummed his fingers on his desk and perused the male before him, dressed in jeans and a sweatshirt with a superhero logo on it of all things. Did today's youth not own proper attire at all?

Compared to Lucifer, dressed in a three-piece suit complete with a tie, the young man looked like a bum. Totally disrespectful, which in some cases was a sin he could appreciate, unless used in his presence. Then it just annoyed him.

At least Adexios' father, Charon, wore a clean and ominous robe, over what, Lucifer preferred not to dwell on. As far as Lucifer knew, only Charon's wife knew what hid under it. A brave female. But back to the son. "I'm displeased with you, Adexios."

Geeky appearance or not, the boy didn't flinch at the rebuke. "My deepest apologies, my lord. I never meant to offend."

Said with perfect sincerity, no lie, he would have spotted it. However, given Lucifer had called the boy in for a personal interview, where was the shaking, the sweat, the groveling, the tears? How was he to properly chastise the boy if he didn't instill fear? Was he losing his touch? Lucifer adopted a more serious mien. "How could you not offend? You lost a boatload of souls. Lost them because you wanted to take a nap!"

Finally a reaction. The young man fidgeted. "I hear they were found."

"But not before they were turned into zombies. Zombies! And not even the useful decaying kind that I can use on the mortal plane to fuck with people. I've got mindless soul zombies. What the fuck am I supposed to do with them now?"

"Rent them out to your Dismembering Punishment Commission?" Adexios offered with a shrug.

Not a bad idea. But Lucifer wasn't about to reward the slacker on the suggestion to bring more coins to his hellacious coffers. "This can't continue," he boomed. "You've capsized I don't know how many of your father's boats. Delayed numerous charters, which caused havoc in processing. You're an utter disappointment when it comes to filling your father's robe."

Adexios shoved at his thick-rimmed glasses and used that moment to gather it seemed his thoughts. Hopefully he also found his wits. "Um, would it help to say, I'm sorry?"

"No, it would not!" Did no one around here grasp the fact Lucifer hated excuses, especially polite ones?

"Oh. How about, I will try to do better?"

A big sigh left Lucifer. The boy truly had none of his father's mysterious and spooky character. "What am I going to do with you, boy? You need a job, but it's obvious you are not a boatman."

"If I might suggest, my lord, perhaps you could find me a spot in the HRD."

"Hell's Revenue Department is already overstaffed as it is and has an extensive waiting list when it comes to employment. It seems the mortal plane has more than its fair share of sinning accountants. No. We need to find you a new job. One that you can't fuck up. Your father tells me you're good with numbers."

"I am, my lord."

"Excellent. Pack a bag."

Ah, the sweet look of shock as the calm and collected geek got hit with the unexpected. "Excuse me?"

"Pack a bag, or not. I don't care, but you will be gone a while."

"Gone where, my lord?"

"Does it matter?" Before the young man could ask more questions—*does he not grasp just who's in charge here?*—Lucifer answered him, gleefully and with a smile full of teeth—filed recently for cosmetic effect. "You are going to voyage into the ninth circle and the wilds."

"The wilds?" Squeaked with proper alarm.

That's more like it. "Yes, the wilds. Trouble is brewing. I can sense it." Feel it with every ounce of his demonic body.

"And you want *me* to find it?"

"Of course not. Given your bumbling antics, you're more likely to aid it than stop it. No, what I want from you is numbers. As in, number of demons available for my army. I know how many I can call in the rings. What I need to know is how many abide in outer parts. And that's where you come in. You will travel to those distant locales and recruit all able-bodied demons and keep track of their numbers."

"Me recruit demons? What makes you think they'll listen to me?"

"I shall give you a Dark Seal."

"Gee, I feel so much better."

Oh ho, was that sarcasm he detected? Finally a hint of disrespectful spirit. "You should. A Dark Seal and a quest from me is a great honor. But I know not all my loyal minions are well behaved. It's what I do so like about them. Given their rambunctious nature, and in my generosity, I am giving you some help. You'll have a companion on your quest."

"Hell's mightiest warrior?"

"You could say that. Only the best for Charon's son." Lucifer smiled, and something in it must have tipped Adexios off because he blanched.

The phone on his desk rang. About time. "Run along now, boy, and pack. Your escort will be along within the next few days to fetch you. You wouldn't want to keep her waiting."

"Her?"

Before Adexios could ask more questions, Lucifer waggled his fingers, sending the boy flying out of his office and slamming the door shut. Let him stew for a while. It would do him some good.

The old style rotary phone on his desk, carved from black ebony—a tusk from a boar-headed, fifteen-foot demon he'd bested in hand-to-hand combat many centuries ago--continued to ring. Lucifer answered. "Finally the cat calls with a status report. You took your sweet time."

"I ran into problems."

Lucifer frowned. Damn the river and that stupid isle. His scrying just couldn't penetrate those areas, which irritated him to no end. How was he supposed to properly spy when handicapped by stupid magical no-go zones?

"What kind of problems? Did the chit give you any trouble? Or was it those meddlesome sirens?" Hot ladies who knew how to show a man a good time. Ah, for the good old days when he didn't have a jealous girlfriend threatening to castrate him if he wandered.

"Neither. We were attacked."

"Attacked? By who?"

"The first attack we believe was orchestrated by the mermaids. Squads of Undines attacked us on the isle."

"How dare those cold fish involve themselves in my affairs. I trust you beat their male drones back."

A snort was Felipe's reply. "They didn't stand a chance. It also convinced the sirens that it was best we leave promptly."

"We? So you have the girl?"

"Yes, I managed to leave the island with Jenny when the second attack occurred."

"Second? You mean someone dared attack you in one of my rings? On my lands?"

"No, it happened while we were sailing on the Styx."

Lucifer made a dismissive noise. "Bah. Sea monsters are always attacking. It's what they're supposed to do."

"Except it wasn't a sea monster. According to the siren piloting the yacht, the cyclone we faced on the Styx was unnatural, and of immense power. We barely survived."

"A magical storm on the Styx?" The news stunned Lucifer. No one understood all the odd rules of magic coursing through the Hell plane, but there was one immutable fact. The Styx was a neutral zone. Yes, monsters flourished in it. Yes, it could be sailed, not without hazard, but when it came to magic and controlling it or the elements surrounding it, attempts fizzled. It was like a magical vacuum existed on the Styx sucking up all attempts. The fact someone not only managed to create a storm, but a super one at that, one aimed at his minions, didn't bode well and just added to his certainty something exciting came this way.

Yay, a war. Or at least something to break up the monotony of punishing wicked souls over and over. After eons of it, a demon needed something to liven things up. Nothing like the possibility of facing dire danger, a mysterious villain, and directing his legions into battle to get his blood pumping. Total boner.

"I gotta go," he said to the cat. "I've got things to do." Such as debauching a certain woman.

"But don't you want to know where we are? And when we'll arrive."

"You're obviously safe, or you wouldn't be calling. You have Jenny still, I assume?"

"Yes, but—"

"Bring her to me as soon as you can. Alive or I'll be using your fur as a rug."

Before Felipe could say another word, Lucifer slapped the phone into its cradle and bellowed, "Gaia!"

He leaned back in his chair, undid his pants, and let his mighty beast spring forth.

He waited.

And waited.

A frown creased his brow. "Woman, where are you?" he yelled again. "I know you can hear me. You're always listening in." Darned female, always sticking her nose in his affairs. She spied almost as well as he did.

This time she answered his call, arriving in a cloud of green sparkles that emitted an obnoxiously fresh-flowered smell that totally clashed with the manliness of his office.

"About time," he grumbled as he waved his erect dick at her.

She gave him and his mighty snake but a cursory glance. "Really, Luc. How many times do I have to tell you that is not sexy?"

"You like it well enough when I use it to plow you."

"After some foreplay. But that…" She waved a dismissive hand in his direction. "Wagging it around? Surely in the thousands of years you've prided yourself on being a lover, you've acquired a more suave method of seduction."

"I thought we were past all that crap," he complained. Wasn't the whole point of dating and fidelity so he could bypass the annoying parts and get right to the fun stuff?

"Just because we're lovers doesn't mean you have to stop trying."

"But all that seduction crap takes time. And I want some nookie now." He gave her his best pout.

She ignored it. "What's this I hear about a new menace heading toward Hell?"

"Nothing to worry your pretty head about, although I do know of another head in need of attention." He tried a winsome smile—which always failed with the ladies, but he kept practicing. He'd seen Felipe and Remy use it, with success he might add. Lucifer just couldn't figure out why his version didn't have the same effect. For some reason, with the exception of Gaia, women either screamed or fainted at the sight of it.

His smile didn't work. His groin waggle didn't merit a glance. And his suggestive leer met with a furrow. "Be serious for a moment. We need to talk about the news Felipe just imparted. Who has the power to mess with the Styx?" mused his girlfriend.

With a big sigh, as Lucifer realized he wouldn't get any coital action until he'd—ugh—had a conversation with the missus, he tucked his equipment back in his pants. "I don't know who has the skill to do such a thing. The sea hag might have, but that crazy cow's been asleep for eons."

"Maybe she woke up?"

"Doubtful. Trust me on this, we'd know if the hag had returned." Although Lucifer did wonder for a moment if the sea hag was capable of shaping magic in her dreams. *Hey, maybe she had a wet dream about her old lover boy, Neptune.* A chuckle-worthy thought but not conducive for the conversation at hand.

Musing aloud, Gaia paced, her green skirts swirling around her trim ankles, ankles that would look so much better draped over his shoulders. "Lilith might have known a spell and been able to muster the power, but she's gone."

Good riddance. Lucifer was still miffed at the pain and suffering that bitch put his daughter, Muriel, through. Not that he'd tell anyone. The Lord of the Pit did not talk about his feelings, and he certainly never admitted to affection, even for the special child born of his and Gaia's loins. "Even if Lilith weren't, without access to the damned souls to power her spells, she wouldn't have the strength either. No one does. The Styx is a magical vacuum."

"Yet someone still managed to conjure a super storm. Someone we obviously don't know. So what are we going to do about it?"

"We?"

"Yes, we," was Gaia's firm response. "We are a team now. Anyone who threatens you, threatens me."

How disgustingly adorable. Lucifer might not need her to defend him but... "Do you know how sexy you are when you act all protective?"

"How sexy?" Gaia asked, whirling to face him in a swirl of green toile.

"Almost makes me want to say the L word sexy."

Her eyes widened, and he bit back a grin. Dare to insult him by claiming he wasn't the king of seduction? Ha. He knew how to please his woman. Say hello to the master of oral.

"You are such a tease." And yet, Gaia still sported a hint of pink in her cheeks.

It seemed his woman needed a little more convincing. "When I take to the field of battle, will you ride with me? I could use you by my side." Not really, but they'd definitely look striking. Him atop his mighty black Hellsteed, her atop her white, single-horned mare.

The HBC—Hell's Broadcasting Corporation and its subsidiaries—would love it. Lucifer always got high ratings when he went all badass.

"You want me by your side. Truly?" She licked her full lips, lips that would look so good wrapped around his cock.

"I wouldn't trust anyone else to guard my flank." And that was the ugly truth. Blech. How he hated honesty, but it served its purpose in this case.

Gaia draped herself on his lap and ran a finger down his chest. "I've always wanted to fight by your side."

"You know we make an awesome duo. Just think, my demons and your army of green, fighting together to save Hell from annihilation. Could there be anything more binding for a couple such as you and I? Will you be my war queen?" He held out his hand, and with a push of power, yanked a treasure from his hidden trove. It shimmered into appearance, a large ring of white gold set with fire diamonds. A tiara fit for a goddess.

"Yes. Oh yes!" squealed Gaia. "I accept your proposal."

Wait a second. She didn't think he meant—

He lost his train of thought as a certain seductress hit the floor between his legs and took him in hand. Well, mouth really. Then he didn't think at all.

Chapter Fourteen

Felipe frowned at the phone.

"What's wrong?" Jenny asked as she exited the bathroom, wrapped in a fluffy towel and while using another to dry her green hair.

"He hung up on me."

"Who did?"

"Lucifer."

"Maybe he was done talking."

"But I'd not gotten to the most important part of my message. He doesn't know about the problem with the portal. Or at least this portal."

A problem that they only heard about once they'd huffed and puffed their way to the top of the cliff following Valasca, who didn't even break a sweat. The bitch. Irrational or not, Jenny hated the toned and tanned warrior. Compared to her, Jenny felt like the ugly cousin. Not that Felipe had done anything to make her feel that way. On the contrary, he didn't really spend any time looking at their escort. But he'd also not tried to cop a peek at her in the shower or kissed her again since the interruption on the beach.

However, back to the portal issue—as opposed to her jealousy one. After their interminable climb and their meeting with Thora, they'd emerged to find a mild state of panic. It seemed the Amazons' portal had collapsed. Just shrunk in on itself and, with a sucking noise, popped out of existence, leaving the warrior women perplexed and them without a quick means of making it to the inner rings.

That combined with everything else meant Felipe felt a need to call Lucifer with a status report.

"Why not call him back?" Jenny suggested as she opened an armoire to find some toga-styled robes hanging, none of them long enough to hide her scaled legs. Legs she couldn't help but realize were in plain view. She'd almost stayed in the bathroom because of them, worried about coming out and Felipe catching his first full-on glimpse of her deformity.

Which is dumb because we've almost had sex a few times. He's run his hand up my leg. Caught glimpses of them and not said a word. However, little peeks were on thing, a full-on introduction to her strangeness another.

Better know now if they were going to deter him from seduction than in the midst of the act. To his credit, he'd not said anything nor did he appear disturbed in the least.

However, exposing them to him, alone, in this room they shared in the guest quarters of the Amazon village was one thing, wandering around with them on display for all of Hell to see, another.

"I've already hit redial twice, and I keep getting a message saying the Lord of Hell is too busy to answer because he's getting some followed by some corny music."

"You're joking," she said as she debated between the white toga dress and the dark grey one.

"Nope. My Lord isn't discreet when it comes to his sex life."

"Sounds like some aunts I know," she muttered, continuing to browse in the hopes of finding an outfit that would cover more of her up.

"I'll wait a bit and try again. Meanwhile, how cool is that about the amulet?"

Now there was something to make her grin. Jenny hadn't placed much faith in it but despite that, hung it around her neck in the faint hope it might help.

They tested it on the first Amazon they came across. Jenny said, "Hello, how are you?", and the servant, who didn't scream or bleed from any orifices, must have thought her a crazy nut for laughing and dancing around her in the hallway saying, "I can talk. Listen to me. I can talk." But as Felipe reassured her, having a reputation for being crazy in Hell wasn't a bad thing.

"This amulet is the best present ever. I just wonder why my aunts never thought of it when I was growing up. It would have been nice to have when I was dating that guy they set me up with."

"What guy?" Felipe growled. His eyes flashed yellow, and Jenny couldn't help but shiver.

Is he jealous? She knew she certainly was. The women in this place were paying way too much attention to her male companion. And she didn't like it. The amulet might not stay around her neck for long if they didn't keep their hands and overt stares to themselves.

Foolish, she knew. On a visceral level, she understood Felipe didn't belong to her. He was much too wild for that. Anything they shared would be, at best, temporary. Yet, for the moment, she couldn't help a sense of ownership.

He was with her. *Which makes him mine.* And given Jenny never grew up with anyone or had any real friends, the concept of sharing wasn't something she understood, or cared to learn about.

Apparently her woolgathering before the open wardrobe didn't go unnoticed. "I seem to detect an issue with the available apparel. Have you decided against getting dressed? Thinking about keeping the towel on? Actually, I've got a better idea, why don't you ditch it altogether?" Felipe practically purred the suggestion.

She shot him a glance over her bare shoulder and found him lounging on the queen-sized bed, hands laced behind his head, lips curved in a grin.

"I'm trying to find something, but the togas are all so short."

"It's known as easy access."

"Easy access for what?" As soon as she asked, she knew. Hot blood rushed to her cheeks, and moisture honeyed her sex as his smile widened.

"Want me to show you?"

Yes. "No. Now's not exactly the time. We have more important things to worry about, don't you think? Such as how we're going to get to this inner ring you keep talking about especially since the portal is broken. We're in the sixth ring according to Valasca."

A negligent wave showed Felipe's nonchalant attitude about their dilemma. "Sixth or ninth, doesn't really matter. A pair of Hellsteeds and a few days' ride and we'll be in the capital barring any incidents."

Her nose wrinkled. "Ride a horse? Isn't that hard?"

"Oh, Jenny," Felipe groaned. "I know you don't mean to, but the things you say…"

"What about them?"

"Are you truly so naïve as to not know how they could be misconstrued?"

No. She'd heard sexual innuendos for most of her life. The sirens weren't exactly subtle. However, this was the first time in her life Jenny realized how her words could have that effect on a man. It was so novel and unexpected. She revised what she'd just said and couldn't help the mischievous curl of her lips. "I guess if anyone has experience in teaching a girl to ride hard things it would be you. Given my inexperience, are you offering to teach me?"

It wasn't the sudden flare of yellow hunger in his eyes that stole her breath but rather the speed with which he sprang from the bed and stalked toward her. And she did mean stalk.

He moved with a loose-limbed grace, an animalistic prowess that literally stole her ability to move, or breathe. Prowling across the space separating them, he stopped before her, his body so close she could feel the heat radiating from him. A heat she wanted to touch.

"You shouldn't say things like that," he said in a raspy voice.

"Why?"

"Because a man might assume you're offering."

She peeked into his smoldering golden gaze. "What if I am?"

"You do realize I'm not the kind of guy who sticks around, right? That while we might have fun now and flirt, ultimately you're a mission. Once I deliver you to Lucifer, we probably won't see each other again."

"If you're telling me this is a one-shot deal, then, yes, I understand. I'm not stupid. I realize a girl like me doesn't have much to offer a man like you."

Her back hit the wall, and his body pressed into hers, unyielding and hard. The violence of the act shocked out an inadvertent gasp.

"Don't say that," he growled.

"Say what?"

"Talk about yourself as if you're less than perfect. I thought we'd already clarified you are rare and precious."

She shrugged. "If you say so."

"I do say so." His fingers gripped her chin and held her facing him, his grip almost punishing. "You. Are. Beautiful. Desirable. A temptation I can't seem to resist."

Nor did he try. His lips crushed hers with a bruising ferocity she welcomed. When he kissed her like that, Jenny could almost believe him and forget her own self-doubts. Forget her past, her mother, the image reflected in the mirror.

Threading her fingers through his silky hair, Jenny lost herself in the kiss. Despite her reply to him that she wasn't looking for anything more than what he was willing to give, a part of her couldn't help but want to pretend that they shared something more. Something special. That she was hugged and kissed by a man who cared for her and would never leave her. A foolish dream, but one she couldn't resist.

It took her enjoyment to a new level, one where she relaxed and lost herself. The towel somehow slipped away as they devoured each other. It left the bare skin of her torso pressing against his. Oh how the heat scorched. How the feel of his naked flesh aroused. The peaks of her breasts tightened into buds, protruding nubs that rubbed against his chest, sending shivers throughout her. Her legs went weak, and she sagged in his embrace, but she didn't fall. His arms tightened around her. Holding her closer, firmer, exciting even more parts, especially a certain damp part, which throbbed and begged for more.

Good thing for the wall at her back. It braced her as his thigh inserted itself between her legs. She couldn't help but grind her sex against his muscled leg, gasping in his mouth at the friction this simple motion placed on her clit. It also made her even wetter.

He sucked in a breath, her breath really, given their lips were sealed. But he didn't pull away or slow down. Instead, he expanded his sensual exploration, dragging his lips across her cheek to the sensitive shell of her ear. Who knew this would prove such an erogenous zone? A shiver went through her at his lick and tug of this surprising spot. A moan slipped from her as her pleasure increased.

Not a word was spoken between them. No false promises made—even if she did think of a few fantasy ones. With their bodies so decadently tangled, their hearts racing in cadence, and bliss surely only moments away, who needed speech when touch could convey things so much more eloquently ... and pleasurably?

His hands skimmed down her body, burning a path of awareness until the tips of his fingers landed on the bared skin of her hips. But they didn't linger there long. He reached behind and cupped the fullness of her bottom, using his new grip to rotate her pelvis so that she received even more pressure from his leg. Firm and bristled with short hairs, it stroked her most intimate part, a delectable friction that had her panting and yearning for more.

She couldn't have said when her hands moved from stroking his hair to gripping his muscled shoulders, but at the increase in stimulation to her clit, she only vaguely noticed she dug her nails into him. Blame him. The tension coiling within her needed, no, make that demanded, she clench something.

Did he sense that? Was that why he removed his thigh, only to replace it with his hand, his evil, wondrous hand with deft fingers that toyed with her swollen nub. Jenny couldn't help but keen in pleasure as he stroked her. Faster and faster he worked his erotic magic, rubbing her clit while she desperately clung to him, panting and keening wordless sounds.

When he stopped his friction, she cried out in protest. "No, don't stop."

"We're not done. Not by a long shot," he purred.

She could have sighed in relief as he slid his finger into her damp sex. Finally, something she could squeeze. Back and forth he seesawed, penetrating her, teasing. And that was all it was. A tease. She needed more. Something thicker, longer…

The distinctive sound of fabric tearing managed to pry her heavy lids open. Directing her gaze down, she was in time to see his cock spring forth. Long and thick, his shaft strained toward her, the head fat and the tip gleaming with a pearl drop of moisture. She couldn't help but reach for it, her thumb rubbing over the silky cap, her sex shuddering as he groaned in pleasure.

She clasped her hand around him, and his hips jerked, pushing his erection through her fingers, and she couldn't help but imagine how it would feel inside her. Apparently, he wanted to know too because he cupped her by the buttocks and hoisted her, the pressure of the wall against her back keeping them from toppling, or her at any rate. She doubted her legs could hold her now.

The head of his cock, so thick with its velvety soft skin, probed her wet sex, taunting her.

While she enjoyed the sensuous rub, she wanted more and found the courage to demand it. "Give it to me."

He chuckled. "Such impatience."

She nipped at his ear. "More like worried about interruptions." Which seemed to always plague them once things got interesting.

"Good point." And with that, he thrust into her, and she let out a happy cry.

He withdrew and plunged deep again then held it. It felt great. He stretched her so nicely. He fit so snugly. But as she wiggled around, she couldn't help but want a little more action from him. "What are you waiting for?"

"Didn't someone want lessons on riding?"

Say what?

"Wrap your legs around my waist."

With pleasure, since it drew him even deeper inside. She'd no sooner locked her ankles around his back than he walked them to the bed. He sat them down, him on the edge of the mattress, her astride him, still penetrated by his cock. Fingers digging into her cheeks, he bounced her.

Oh my.

Again. Up and down he jostled her, the jolt each time she seated herself pushing him in far, far enough to touch something sensitive inside. A sweet spot that made her gasp. It also caused her channel to squeeze around his shaft, his very thick shaft.

Long gone were any previous misconceptions and the unsatisfying experience from her past lover. This was sex. This was pleasure. This was ... oh my freaking—

She never did finish that thought. Couldn't, not when he began to bounce and grind her faster and faster, sucking all her breath at the intensity of the ecstasy, draining her of coherent thought, coiling and building a wave of delight until it burst, a cascading, orgasmic wave that crashed through her. Swept her along for a blissful journey that saw her tilting her head back and letting out a scream of pure joy.

How utterly glorious.

And still he thrust, her atop him riding as he reached his own pinnacle and crested, triggering a second smaller orgasm, which didn't draw forth a scream but a sigh of utter contentment.

As she collapsed in his arms, not even the distant screaming—*oops, I guess I should have put the amulet back on after my shower*—could diminish her pleasure in what they'd indulged.

Even more marvelous, she discovered sex with her ankles locked around his shoulders and on her knees from behind also had its merits.

Luckily for the inhabitants of the rooms around them, she remembered to wear her magical talisman during those pleasurable bouts, else the fortress might have found itself short a few inhabitants in the morning given her enthusiastic shouts.

Chapter Fifteen

The following morning saw no change in the status of the portal. It still wasn't working, and none of the Amazons, not even the elder, could fathom why.

But Felipe harbored his own suspicions. How timely, and inconvenient, that just as they required the quickness of a portal, the closest one available was suddenly nonoperational. Only idiots believed in coincidences.

Calls to the Dark Lord still went unanswered, and the voicemail he'd left didn't merit a return call. It seemed Felipe would have to take Jenny overland, and lucky him—NOT!—he wouldn't do so alone.

No amount of argument would sway Valasca from traveling with them. Tasked with going to the capital to relay firsthand the problem with the portal and to demand—as if the independent warriors would stoop to asking—for a fix to the problem meant Felipe would have to temper his acts and words to Jenny.

As if he even knew what he'd say. They'd spent a glorious night. More than glorious. They'd connected sexually, but Felipe, actually his cat, had almost done more than that. The bloody feline had tried to mark her! He'd even gone so far as to drop fang during the act. Thank fuck she'd not noticed. But still, that kind of lack of control was freaky to say the least.

What happened to living the single life? He'd thought his inner beast content with their lifestyle. Wenching and adventuring. It was the dream of so many, and he loved it, didn't he?

Never mind he hated going home to an empty apartment. Forget the fact that he begged meals at Ysabel's table more often than was seemly for a tom his age. And he'd kill anyone who dared to remark on the fact that he smiled whenever he saw fathers out and about with their young, tossing them in the air to catch as the tots giggled, or how he envied those teaching their sons life lessons such as how to pee in the alleys without getting it on their feet.

Living his life as he chose without anyone to answer to, no one to harangue him about leaving his socks on the floor, and enjoying a different flavor of pussy whenever the fancy struck, that was the true dream. So what if, at times, it was lonely, and he felt … unsatisfied? Alcohol had ways of minimizing that effect.

And why was he even worrying about what he'd say to Jenny? She'd barely spared him a glance since they'd left the privacy of the room they'd shared. Her casual ignoring should have relieved him. Instead, he was kind of offended.

Usually, he couldn't keep women off him. It was why he preferred their place to his. They couldn't track him down once he slunk off. So shouldn't he rejoice in the fact that Jenny wasn't clinging to him like a bloody hellyfish? That she didn't give him woeful hellhound eyes or pout with that delectable lower lip?

Just a day ago, he might have blamed her lack of response on her fear of causing harm with her voice. However, her needed bubble of silence was a thing of the past. With the amulet the shaman—or was that shawoman?—gave Jenny, she blossomed and chattered away with the Amazons, asking questions, laughing, and smiling wider than he'd ever seen. He guessed the burden of having people kill themselves when she spoke would feel onerous, and he was glad she'd found a reprieve from her curse. He just wished he could have been the one to bring her such joy and he glowered as she gossiped animatedly with everyone but him.

Despite her fear about riding, Jenny took well to the saddle. He'd like to think the practice the night before atop him—fuck, how glorious she looked with her hair streaming down her back, her eyes half lidded as she rode him in wild abandon—had something to do with it, but the gentle Hellmare they'd given her might have played a minor part. The older beast plodded along, the fires of her youth tempered to coals. Not so the horse they gave him. The damned stallion pranced and danced, fighting him every step of the way.

The antics of his steed amused Valasca, who didn't bother hiding her snicker every time his damned beast tossed its head and, with smoke curling from its nostrils, reared in an attempt to jolt him off. Like that would happen. Felipe grimly held on, fists wrapped around the reins, knees pressed tight against its sides. He won, but not for one minute did he let his guard down.

For Hell, the day was surprisingly nice. The sifting ash wasn't too heavy in this part of the ring, just a light dusting that a gentle breeze carried away. The road, more a worn trail of compact dirt, remained clear of obstacles and bandits. They made good time, such good time they ignored the accommodations in town and pressed on, more because Valasca goaded him than because of a pressing need for speed.

"Does the soft kitty need a bed to sleep?"

Pride wouldn't let him scream "Yes!" So on they forged, making camp by the road and relying on the loaned bedrolls and a fire they built to stay comfortable because, Hell or not, when night fell, while the temperature remained pretty much the same, the darker creatures of the night woke and roamed. Fire often proved a deterrent but, more importantly, if stoked with the right fuel, gave them light, a light that glinted off any watching eyes.

The first night passed without incident—and no sex. Which was fine with Felipe. Since when did he go back for seconds? Then again, other than his foster mother, how often could he say he'd spent more than a few hours in a woman's company? Jenny was the first he'd ever really gotten to know, and like.

They each took a turn on watch, Jenny getting first watch, the safest one. The Amazon gave him second, where he spent too much time checking on his green-haired temptress as she slept—her hand tucked under her cheek, a vision of loveliness he longed to debauch.

Third watch was Valasca's.

While off in the distance things rustled, howled, growled and in general made their presence known, nothing came too close. A shame. Fresh meat for breakfast would have been nice.

When morning came, they made do with dried rations and continued on, Jenny chatting with Valasca, him bringing up the rear, brooding. Sulking. Depressed.

And not doing a good job of hiding it.

When they stopped at a river to refresh themselves and their mounts, Valasca broached it while Jenny kept an eye on the horses, who lapped hungrily from the riverside.

"Why does the kitty look like he's lost his favorite toy?"

"I don't know what you're talking about."

"Of course you do. Only a blind idiot or, in this case, a naïve one called Jenny, wouldn't notice the fact you're upset about something. I'll bet I can guess what."

As if he'd admit he pined after a woman. "I'm not upset, just perplexed that after the problems we had leaving the isle, Jenny's enemies seem to have given up."

Shading her eyes so she could better stare at the road behind them, Valasca replied, "Perhaps they realized it was futile to stop her."

"Doubtful." The storm they survived was no minor thing. Why launch such a major attack unless they meant serious business? Felipe's gut didn't trust the ease of their trip. His gaze strayed over to where Jenny stroked the mane of her mare. No way was he letting her out of his sight. "I think her enemies are just biding their time. We need to stay alert and watch for a possible ambush."

"From where?"

Valasca gestured at the flat plains around them. This part of the circle bore little in way of cover, the dryness of the land and the sparseness of habitation meaning they could see for almost miles around.

"I'm not saying they're going to attack in the next minute, just that it's possible and we should remain vigilant."

"I'm always on guard. And you are using the obvious to ignore my question. Why are you moping? It is plain to see you desire Jenny. So why aren't you doing something about it?"

Plain to everyone but Jenny apparently. "Well, for one, I'm not into an audience."

Valasca snorted. "As if I'm interested in watching."

"Still, I think Jenny would prefer privacy."

"Lame excuse. You're a player. Players always find ways to have sex, no matter the circumstance."

True. "I don't want her to get the wrong idea. As you noticed, Jenny is kind of inexperienced when it comes to men. While we did have sex that one time back in your village, I'm worried that repeat encounters will have her thinking the wrong thing."

"So you abstain so as to not hurt her feelings?"

He nodded.

"Admirable, but stupid."

"How is it stupid to not want to lead her on?"

"The girl is already taken with you. Whether you have sex or not, that won't change, so all you're doing is punishing both of you. Actually, this might be worse. When you part, she'll only have her one encounter with you to remember. To place on a pedestal. Whereas, having sex numerous times would allow her to sate her attraction to you, notice you have faults, and when the time comes, possibly feel a sense of relief that there's an easy way to end things."

"Hold on a second, are you saying she needs to have copious sex with me so she can, in effect, discover what a jerk I am and get bored of my technique?"

"Yes. It's what happens with all my lovers. The first time you fuck, it's got the element of newness. The second time, it scratches an itch that tries to recapture that feeling. By the third and fourth, you're going through the motions. By the fifth, you don't want to be bothered by what he wants, you just need a quick release."

"And by the sixth?"

"He's dead."

"Dead?" Felipe snorted. "Let me guess. Bereft at getting dumped, the guys kill themselves rather than face a life without you? Is someone a little conceited?"

"No, they're dead because I give them an impossible quest to get back into my pants to prove their love to me, a quest they fail."

"That seems fucking cold."

"Not my fault they're weak. If they were strong enough to be my mate, they would be able to accomplish the task I set them."

"And just what task is that?"

Before he could find out, Jenny's shrill scream interrupted. He glanced at the river, only to realize that while he'd conversed with the Amazon, Jenny had moved farther downstream, just out of sight.

Dammit.

They both took off at a run, Valasca drawing her sword, him stripping clothes.

At Jenny's second shrill cry for help, his cat burst out of his skin and roared. A horse whinnied, a panicked cry cut off short and replaced by a more ominous silence. The thin bushes bordering the sluggish moving river couldn't completely screen the unfolding drama.

I am so fucking stupid. When Jenny declared she could water the horses on her own, he'd checked the riverbank. He'd sniffed the air. Perused the ground for tracks. Seen no sign of danger. None. Or at least none on the surface.

He'd not taken into account that the shallow river, waist deep at the most, could hide the enemy. In his defense, this far inland from the ocean, he'd not expected an aquatic attack.

A rookie mistake. A deadly miscalculation. A problem he needed to rectify was his final thought before he soared through the air intent on tackling the biggest problem—which wasn't the eight Undines surrounding Jenny and the two still living horses. Nope. He was going after the electrical eel that sizzled and sparked as it wound its sinuous coils around the corpse of Jenny's poor mare.

This is going to sting. And it did. He landed on the coil closest to him, the electrifying zing coursing through his limbs and making his fur stand on end.

Me-fucking-ow!

Pain or not, he dug his claws into the slimy scales coating the serpent's body. The creature didn't like this at all and hissed at him. The head, with its ruffled fin atop its crown and one lidless eye, swung in his direction. The mouth opened wide, revealing pointed teeth.

That, Felipe could have handled. It was the appearance of the second eel, which he didn't note until it whipped its tail around him, pinning him in its coils, that proved problematic.

Fuck. He hated it when his dinner ganged up on him. *There goes another of my lives.*

Chapter Sixteen

Ever since the night she and Felipe spent together in the Amazon village, Jenny felt different. She couldn't have exactly said why or how. It partially had to do with the amulet the Amazons gave her, an amulet to nullify the effects of her voice, meaning for the first time in her life she could speak freely and without fear. Her new attitude could have resulted from the night she spent with Felipe, an evening of discovery and sensual delight that opened her eyes to a whole new realm.

I now see why my aunts enjoy their sailors so much.

But those two acts alone weren't the only things affecting her newfound confidence. She'd left home and faced danger. Survived. More than survived, she'd helped Felipe when he would have drowned. She'd done that. And she took the first step in teasing him into her bed. She'd taken charge of her sexuality and discovered pleasure.

She learned to ride a horse and was now discovering Hell. *Finally, I'm doing stuff and truly living.* But she wanted to do more. She knew Felipe and Valasca regarded her as someone in need of coddling. On a certain visceral level, she understood they didn't mean to come across as patronizing, but they did, which was why she was determined to show them she could handle herself.

She insisted on taking a turn at night watch. Yeah, they gave her the first one, and yes, she knew neither slept while she kept guard, but it was a start. She insisted on caring for her own horse. Helping with the fire. And, now, watering their steeds.

It should have been a simple task. Take the horses to water. Show a little independence—after Felipe prowled up and down the shoreline searching for predators.

Still, after declaring the area monster free, he'd left her alone. A small victory. Wouldn't it figure something would rise from the river to fuck up her plans?

At first, when she'd seen the lone eye blinking at her through the watery current, she'd paid it no mind. Waterways held life; that was an immutable fact. What they shouldn't hold, though, was two squads of Undine warriors leaping up brandishing their coral swords, nor a giant electrical eel so far from the ocean.

As a singer, not a fighter, she did what she'd learned during her first self-defense class with Teles. She screamed. Then waited for things to fall over dead or start clawing at their eyes. Only when the sea-warriors slogged toward her, undaunted by the current, and not bleeding from any orifices, did she recall the stupid amulet, the one around her neck making her most effective weapon obsolete.

Before she could fumble it out of the bodice of her gown for removal, the first Undine was upon her, the eel was inching toward her mare, and she was not too frightened or stupid to call for help.

Her second scream was answered by a roar, as Felipe came bounding into view all striped

141

fur, teeth, and claws, too late though for her poor horse, who'd succumbed to the sea serpent.

Valasca arrived a moment after, sword and dagger in hand, yelling a battle cry. It wasn't long before the Undines began to drop dead from the deadly action of her spinning and arcing blades. The way the Amazon wielded them as an extension of herself was utterly fascinating, but Jenny couldn't afford to watch, not when Felipe was in danger.

The idiot, with no thought to the fact electricity could hurt and, in strong enough doses, kill, tackled the serpent. The Undines occupied with the Amazon, and the stallion intent to stomp and indulge in his own fair share of mayhem, Jenny finally managed to slip the thong holding the amulet off. She pocketed the talisman and darted between the bodies into the warm river waters, seeing the advantage finally in the short toga as the skirts weren't getting water logged.

Poor Felipe, his red-and-black-striped fur alternated between matted wet and standing at frizzled attention from the electrical discharge of the second eel, which wound its body around him.

Despite his limbs getting pinned, he wasn't giving up though. His teeth, longer than her forearm she'd swear, did their best to ravage the flesh binding him, but she could tell he weakened, the combination of squeezing, lack of oxygen, and zaps taking its toll.

"Brace yourself," was the only warning she gave before opening her mouth to sing. She could only hope in her desire to save her friends—and one-time lover—she didn't accidentally kill them.

Notes burst free. Bright and colorful things when in her mouth that twisted and darkened as they hit the open air. She could almost see the deadly vibrations of her song as she crooned the words to a melody she'd learned at Molpe's knee. It took a moment for the effect to hit, and despite the lack of true ears on the eels, her ability remained true.

The deadly sound waves hit the serpents. Their heads rocketed straight up on their sinuous necks. Their eyes took on a glazed look, and they wobbled. A low hissing noise of air escaping deflated them, and they slumped, loosening their grip. Felipe snarled and slashed his way free as Jenny continued to sing.

The serpents plopped into the water, dead or unconscious, she didn't care which. Either way the current took them, sucked them into its watery depths, and swept them away.

Shaking his fur, Felipe grumbled and growled as he stalked his way to shore, the scent of singed fur following him.

With him safe, she whirled to help Valasca. But there was no help needed there anymore.

Between her deadly blade work and Jenny's voice, of the attacking Undines, none remained standing, although a few did twitch, but not for long as Valasca took her dagger to them, slitting their throats.

Jenny didn't protest this savagery. When it came to survival, as Aunt Thelxiope always said, "Never leave the enemy alive because it would suck to die at his blade later on out of a misplaced sense of pity."

Of more pressing concern was the blood running from the Amazon's nose and ears. Jenny halted her song mid note, the sudden silence almost deafening after the adrenaline rush of the melody.

"Are you okay?" she asked the first female friend she'd ever truly had.

"I'll be fine. You pack quite a powerful voice in that little body of yours. Good thing Thora gave me a talisman of my own and weaved a spell into our horses bridles. Otherwise, I and our remaining mounts would have probably joined our slimy friends here."

"Sorry."

Valasca winced. "Don't be. That's a fine weapon you've got there, although now that we've taken care of the threat, mind putting the charm back on?"

"Of course." Feeling foolish, Jenny fumbled with the leather thong, slipping it over her head and letting the stone dangle between her breasts.

With a twitch of her head toward Felipe who stalked the shoreline still in his feline shape, Valasca asked, "So how come the cat's not affected?"

The cat in question approached and nudged Jenny's shoulder, almost knocking her over. She reached out to scrub the fur between his ears, glad he seemed none too worse for wear. "Aunt Molpe thinks he's tone-deaf."

"So am I. Or so my friends claim anytime I try to sing."

Jenny laughed. "Not that kind of tone-deaf. For some reason, either because of his shifter status or something else, my magic and that of the sirens doesn't seem to affect him. He doesn't hear the command or ugliness in the music. He hears what I hear."

"Which is what? Because I have to admit, it didn't sound like music." Valasca shuddered. "It was like a giant pressure built in my head, each note pushing and pushing against my brain."

Jenny grimaced. "You're not the first to say that, and yet when I sing I hear—"

"Beauty," supplied Felipe, who'd flipped into his man shape while they talked.

He truly was deaf when it came to music. Jenny almost snorted. Despite what she believed she heard, she wasn't stupid enough to think or believe there was anything beautiful about her deadly music.

But who cared about Felipe's odd view when he stood there in the buff surveying the carnage. The man possessed a truly wicked body. A body she so wanted to touch again. If only he'd not made it so clear their night of pleasure was the only night. He seemed adamant about there being no repeat. A shame because she really, really would have enjoyed exploring the new erotic world she'd discovered a bit more. It would give her a benchmark to aim for in the future as she began her new life.

Perhaps if I made it clear to him that I won't cling or expect anything, he might be willing to give it another go.

All great ideas, if only her newfound courage would allow her to voice them. But, given Felipe was busy leading their two remaining mounts away from the bloodbath and Valasca wouldn't be far behind, she should probably choose a different time.

Regrouping, they planned their next step. "With only the two horses, we need to make a decision," said Valasca. "And the most logical one is to let you have both mounts while I walk back to my village to get a new one."

"Don't be silly," interrupted Felipe. "It will take you too long, and you need to get word to the capital about the portal issue. Especially if it's a widespread one. I've got a better idea. My horse is big and strong while Jenny here's just a wee thing. We'll double up. She can ride in front of me on the saddle, but from now on, no more camping or stopping by bodies of water. I think we've seen enough proof that danger is still stalking her and, given this most recent desperate act, not afraid to let us know."

A curt nod came from Valasca. "Agreed. From now on, we will refresh ourselves in towns and hamlets. Even if the guard is corrupt, they will not allow sea denizens to kidnap or stand in the way of the Dark Lord's minions."

"Yes to the first part, and as for the second part, I won't let anyone take Jenny. She's my mission, and I will get her to the capital."

Sincerity rang in his voice. What a shame it just wasn't the words she'd have preferred to hear like, *I won't let anyone hurt her because she's mine.* Which, on second thought, was exactly why Felipe feared anything more than a one-night stand. Jenny decided to keep that to herself if she ever did get the guts to broach them having sex again. If he thought for one moment she might have emotions for him, he'd never touch her again.

And I do so like it when he touches me. Even innocuously, such as now. Yes, his stallion was big, but the saddle itself was not, which meant she had to more or less sit sideways on his lap, her legs dangling off his thigh, holding on to the pommel with his chest at her back.

He didn't hold her at all. Didn't attempt to cuddle or whisper sweet nothings in her ear. Heck, he didn't even nuzzle her hair, but Jenny hid a secret smile because, despite his outward appearance of nonchalance, he couldn't hide the very distinct and hard erection under her bottom.

Perhaps convincing him won't be so hard after all.

Chapter Seventeen

They paused their journey around the dinner hour, the town, if you could call it that with its ramshackle buildings and mortal realm Western look, boasting a rowdy inn. Felipe could have kissed the innkeeper when he claimed he had only two rooms left.

A more honorable man would have told the women to take the larger of the two to share. He wasn't that man. *Jenny's my responsibility.* A great excuse. One even his cat agreed with. *Mine.*

He'd thought he might have to argue more, though, to get Jenny to join him. He even had his speech prepared: *"It will be safer if you're with me so I can protect you."* And, *"I can handle your voice if you need to remove your amulet."* Or his favorite, *"I'm told I'm a great back scrubber."*

In the end all he had to say was, "We should share a room." And her prompt reply was, "Yes."

First, though, they needed sustenance. His belly growled, especially as he could smell roasted something turning over the spit within the big hearth. What the giant basted carcass once was he didn't care to dwell on. In Hell, meat was meat, no matter what—or who—it came from.

Seated at a table in a corner, his back against the wall, Jenny beside him and Valasca on the other side, he idly watched the patrons as he sipped some awful frothy grog. While alcohol flourished through the nine circles, the quality diminished the farther out one went.

The crowd was much what he'd expect—demons, some damned souls, buxom waitresses, and a few cloaked individuals attempting to blend in but standing out like a sore, swollen dick after a night spent with nymphs.

It was never hard to spot visitors to Hell's circle. They flinched or jumped at loud noises. Their hands strayed often to their waists and their weapons—swords being the arsenal of choice given firearms weren't the most reliable, given the ash and strange magics of Hades often jammed the weapons. Many an idiot thought they could prove the exception and brought a gun to battle, which, in turn, meant there was a thriving trade in eye patches and artificial limbs.

Felipe didn't sense any danger from those present, not even the ogre with the spiked club who sat on the floor, chewing on a haunch almost as big as Jenny. Again, the whole don't-question-what-it-was scenario.

What appeared normal to him, though, was new territory for Jenny.

She leaned close to him and whispered, "Are you sure we're safe here?"

Again, a gentleman would have answered, "Yes." Felipe however replied, "Probably not, so stick close."

Not entirely untrue. She was safest by his side. Did their thighs need to rub as an added precaution? Probably not, but he didn't feel a need to point that out.

Their serving wench arrived with a platter laden with food. She made sure to bend over, way over, as she placed the offering before them. Her plentiful tits practically fell out of her loose-necked blouse. Felipe ignored the clear invitation.

Despite his earlier vow not to go back for seconds with a certain green-haired temptress, he'd since revised that plan. *Sorry but I've got more pleasurable pursuits in mind for the evening.*

Although he didn't show any interest in the wench, Jenny, however, noticed. It also seemed she had a cutting tongue, even when wearing her amulet. "You should take your seamstress to task for making you such an ill-fitting top."

"Say what?" The dark-haired waitress frowned at Jenny's rebuke.

A smile threatened to curve Felipe's lips, a smirk he restrained. Valasca didn't bother, and she snorted. "What my friend here is trying to say is you're being a slut in front of her man, and she doesn't appreciate it."

Felipe meant to reply, but Jenny beat him to it. "He's not my man."

Forget the fact it was pretty much what he would have said, it galled him to hear it come from her mouth.

The waitress, clearly not too bright, probably because she'd drunk too much of the brain-melting grog over the years, thought she should take offense.

"I ain't a slut. I'm a lusty girl who can't help it if men find me attractive. And if he's not her man, why does she give a shit what I'm wearing? I'll bet the fellow sitting with you likes it. Don't you, honey?" The wench then proceeded to flop onto his lap and, before he could say, "Don't involve me," had smothered his face in her cleavage.

Ugh. As if he'd want to sniff the sweat and unbathed flesh of someone so crass. Woman or not, Felipe didn't have a problem shoving the waitress from his lap onto the floor. What he didn't have a hand in and couldn't explain was why he could suddenly scent the unmistakable brine of the sea.

Had their enemies tracked them here?

A low hum vibrated the air and rose in pitch. A damp breeze, smelling of wild, frothing waves filled the air. Felipe glanced to his side and saw Jenny standing, her eyes a blue storm, her hair a tumbling cascade of living, writhing strands, and her lips parted on a note that, had she not worn the amulet, would have probably decimated everyone within the bar.

Felipe recognized her emotion for what it was. Jealousy. While in the past, he'd avoided women who dared to display it on his behalf—again, the whole don't-cling-to-me thing which he abhorred—on Jenny, it was sexy. More than sexy, hot, arousing, and cock hardening.

It took a patron shouting, "Girl fight! Get the oil!" for him to realize Jenny's public display of her powers, and killing of an employee or, in the waitress's case as a damned soul, painful maiming or zombiefying probably wouldn't go over well.

People tended to remember those things and gossip about them. With their enemies obviously tracking them, Felipe should put a stop to it.

I will, in a second. Right after Jenny, who'd somehow made it off the bench they shared, Valasca having cleared the way, stopped stalking, well more like floating as if on an undulating wave of air, toward the no longer so brazen waitress.

"I'm sorry," babbled the wench. "I'll keep my hands off him."

Jenny didn't reply, just lifted her arms and uttered another note, one high enough to make everyone wince. Again, thank fuck for the amulet. That was a definite ear bleeder if he'd ever heard one, and that was from someone who was tone-deaf.

Only once the waitress fled, screeching out the door, did Jenny lower her arms and her feet touched the floor. Fluffing her hair, she did a slow pivot in the now silent bar, her eyes still a blazing blue. She smiled, sweetly. "Anyone else care to maul my companions?"

The remaining females in the place studiously ignored him after that, to the point that Felipe couldn't even get a refill. Valasca snickered throughout the entire meal while Jenny ate with silent serenity. As for Felipe, he found himself hungry, but not for what the innkeeper offered as fare. What he wanted was pink, honeyed, and sitting right beside him.

Without further incident, they made it to their room, bidding Valasca goodnight at the door as she entered the chamber across the hall from them.

Only once the door shut behind them did Felipe loose a chuckle. "Maul? You know flirting isn't a crime?"

"I wouldn't call what she did flirting," was Jenny's sassy reply as she dropped her cloak onto the rickety chair in the corner.

"What would you know of flirting?"

Prowling the room, for what he couldn't have said, she paused and tossed him a coy look over her shoulder, the bare one that peeked from the toga she wore. "I know that there's no need to be so obvious."

"So you think it better if men and women play games? Dance around what they both need instead of coming right out and stating it?"

"Sometimes."

"But what if their time together is limited?" he asked, loosening his belt and dropping it along with the dagger the Amazons had loaned him onto the floor with a solid thump.

"Then perhaps a more direct approach is appropriate, but still, there's flirting, and then there's seducing."

"Oh really? And just how would you go about seducing?"

A smile. One, slow, sensuous smile with a subtle lick of her lips, a tilt of her head that set her hair rippling, and one finger tracing a line between her breasts down the fabric of her gown, stopping just short of her mound.

He swallowed. He throbbed. How he hungered.

"Perhaps you're right," she whispered softly.

"About what?"

"Why flirt when I can be direct?"

With a slowness and grace he tracked with his eyes, her fingers went to the clasp at her shoulder, holding the single strap in place. A strap that she unbuttoned. A quick flick that sent her robe tumbling to the floor in a pile, leaving her in only a pair of plain panties. Moist panties. Damp with a desire he could smell ... and wanted to taste.

"I want you, Felipe."

Such simple words, words he'd heard dozens of times before, yet from her, they affected him strangely. They warmed him and aroused him. They made him forget all the reasons he'd given himself to stay away from her. He couldn't have said how he crossed the room. He just suddenly found himself before her.

But when he would have kissed her, she placed a finger on his lips. "Not this time. Kissing is for lovers and by your own admission, we are not lovers, simply two beings in need of contact."

Yes, lots of contact. Naked contact.

She read his mind because she dropped to her knees, her hands tugging his breeches, pulling them down his corded thighs. At her urging, he stepped out of them and stripped off his shirt, baring himself to her view.

She sighed as she gazed upon him. "You truly have a magnificent body. But I'm sure you already know that."

He did, yet hearing it from her made him swell, not just his chest in pride but his cock in eagerness.

She took him in hand, literally, her fingers wrapping around his aching shaft, squeezing him in her grip. He couldn't help but watch as she leaned forward to kiss the tip of his cock. A simple peck, yet he shuddered. Then he groaned as she licked him, running her tongue from the cap to the root and then back again. Lithe, wet strokes that explored his length and had his legs trembling. Attempting to regain some control, Felipe exhaled. She lightly bit the tip of his cock. He let out a strangled sound and couldn't help but tangle his fingers into the silky curls of her hair.

Good thing he'd found an anchor because Jenny next took him into her mouth, sucking his swollen head before bringing him in deep. His cock pulsed at the moist sensation of her mouth's suction. But it was the sharp edge of her teeth dragging on his tender skin that had him purring.

In and out she slid his shaft, her cheeks hollowed as she suctioned him, her mouth moist and welcoming. It felt so fucking good. Add to that her happy moans of enjoyment and he found himself approaching the brink much too quickly. He fought to hold back.

Extremely pleasurable or not, he wasn't about to blow in her mouth. With regret, he popped his rod free of her mouth, almost going crossed eyed at her mewl of disappointment. He drew her to a standing position, and despite her assertion only lovers should kiss, he ignored that. He wanted a taste. So he did. He kissed her passionately, and she replied back in kind. When her lips parted, he took full advantage, his tongue sneaking into her mouth to dance wetly with hers.

Pressed between their bodies, his cock pulsed against the skin of her lower belly, a pressing reminder that it wanted attention. Despite her initially taking charge of the situation, Felipe took over. Whirling her to face the bed, he had them shuffle a few feet before he placed a hand in the middle of her back to bend her over.

"Brace yourself," he gruffly ordered.

She placed her palms flat on the mattress, her buttocks pointed temptingly in the air still covered by the scrap of fabric the Amazons called panties.

He called them a nuisance, and they were in his way. Not for long. A single tug was all it took to tear them away and reveal her pink center, moist and inviting. He couldn't resist a lick.

She squirmed as he let his tongue dance along her cleft. He purred, unable to hide his pleasure at her evident enjoyment. The soft rumble vibrated against her sensitized sex, and she cried out, a shudder wracking her body.

"Felipe." She sighed his name, and he almost came. Siren or not, when she spoke, it affected him.

He licked her some more, would have loved to have licked her until she came against his lips, but his gums ached as he fought his feline's desire to bite. To mark. To claim…

He mustn't lose himself or forget himself in the moment. They were two fleshly beings in need, not lovers. No matter how right it felt.

But tell that to his cat. He took the temptation away, standing behind her as his fingers slid between her shimmering thighs. Wetting them in the slickness of her sex, he then rubbed them against her clit, circling and pinching the swollen nub until she rocked back against him with wordless cries.

She sat on the edge of orgasm. It was time. He thrust his cock into her, a firm stroke that sheathed him in one swift motion. His fingers dug into the perfect roundness of her ass as her channel clung to his shaft like a velvety glove. Hot, wet, and tight, she squeezed him as he pumped in and out of her.

Her panting cries grew as erratic as her breathing, and she joined him in rocking their bodies; he thrust in as she pushed back, driving him deep until he slammed himself into her welcoming flesh.

"Harder," she cried.

He listened.

"Faster," she begged.

He obeyed.

"Felipe," she yelled as she came, an orgasm he shared. How could he not when her channel fisted and milked his cock, waves of her bliss shuddering through her? He roared as he spurted hotly within her. His fingers scratched her flesh as his whole body went rigid, but she didn't seem to mind the pain, not if the second shuddering climax that went through her was any indicator.

She collapsed face first on the bed, breathing hard. He couldn't help but drape himself atop her naked back, unwilling to lose the closeness. *Not yet.*

She giggled.

He frowned. "What's so funny?"

"I guess I'm not so different from the waitress downstairs after all. I just chose to maul you in private."

He could have pointed out the many differences between them, such as the fact the wench would have gotten a gold coin and a polite boot after giving him head while Jenny … sweet Jenny got to pant again and share his bed. As for the cuddling in his arms? He blamed that on the lumpy mattress.

Chapter Eighteen

The following morning, Jenny did her best to return to her aloofness of before with Felipe. It didn't quite work. For one thing, every time she glanced his way, she couldn't help the heat that coursed through her limbs. All too well, her body remembered how he touched, kissed, seduced. Oh, how it wanted more.

As if he knew his effect, he'd toss her a cocky grin or sneak a pinch to her bottom. But she got him back when they shared his Hellsteed's saddle, subtly rubbing his groin, leaving him in a state of perpetual arousal. He growled in her ear.

"If we didn't have company…"

She murmured back, "Prude. My aunts say having an audience is like extra foreplay."

Audacious words, which she didn't quite mean and trusted he wouldn't act upon. He didn't, but not out of a sense of modesty. "If I weren't afraid of another attack, I'd totally prove you wrong."

Distracting or not, neither could resist the teasing touches. The only thing they did avoid was any talk of the future or what happened between them. Attraction and lust, and the satiation of them, were all they allowed. As their journey took them farther into Hell, the call of the sea but a distant memory left far behind, they spent many nights in strange beds. It became almost a game when they hit the inns, stabling their mounts and refreshing themselves with food and drink at choking speed before escaping to their room, to Valasca's amusement.

But Jenny didn't mind the haste, not when it meant such pleasure.

They spent days on the dusty roads, encountering few other travelers, most giving them a wide berth, especially when Felipe swapped into his feline shape to roam and scout. A magnificent beast, she never tired of watching his graceful prowl as he slunk through the wilderness, popping in and out of sight, the impressive gleam of his saber teeth deterring predators from attack, both the two-legged and four-legged type.

The striped feline with soft fur was a natural-born hunter who delighted in bringing her bloody gifts. They, in turn, used those offerings to pave their way at the inns, partaking of the juicy fresh meat—which gave her and her temporary lover the stamina needed to endure their vigorous activities at night.

As for ambushes and attacks, whoever the culprit was determined to hunt her before seemed to have given up or couldn't find them. But just in case, they took extra caution when they came upon bodies of water, Jenny holding back until Felipe had ascertained them free of danger.

As with all good things, however, their journey eventually came to an end. Or almost. They finally came across a town large enough to boast a portal, a big one too with access to all the rings. It seemed only the portal in the Amazon village was affected, or so they surmised when they entered the fourth ring's bustling marketplace to find their method of traveling the rings intact and working fine.

It was also where Valasca decided to part ways with them.

"According to the merchants, the portal at the compound began working again the day after our departure. Just another vagary of the magic in Hell."

"So you're going home then?" Jenny asked, sad to see her go.

"I will, once I've gathered some supplies. No use in wasting this trip."

"I'll miss you." She certainly would. Valasca offered a refreshing female viewpoint of this new world she found herself in, and her warrior ways were an example that strength came in many forms. Some physical or, like Jenny, metaphysical.

"I could stick with you another day if you think you might need me?"

As if Felipe would admit he needed help. Jenny had grown to understand a lot about the hellcat during their journey. She knew he harbored a lot of pride and that he preferred to be alone, even when on a mission.

It was why she kept guarding her heart. Despite her whimsical fantasy that this magnificent man would grow to care for her, she wasn't foolish enough to believe he'd change his lifestyle to keep her.

However, telling herself to not get attached and actually not allowing it to happen? She feared she'd already failed. *But at least when he leaves, I'll have whatever new adventure awaits me under Lucifer's rule.* And if she didn't like it, she could always return home to her aunts.

Only as a last resort, though. If there was one thing Jenny had discovered, it was she enjoyed the adventure of not knowing what lay ahead and the adrenaline of battle, even against mundane creatures in the wild. She looked forward to the discovery of the new towns and people she encountered. She even got used to the leering stares and ribald remarks—she especially enjoyed them when Felipe reacted with a snarl or a growl.

With a final hug, Valasca and her mount melted into the crowds that streamed into the vast marketplace.

The stallion she and Felipe sat upon lurched as he tugged the reins, their destination in a different direction. Just beyond the outskirts of town, a circular archway of crumbling stone awaited, each of the portals a swirling, multi-colored whirlpool.

Felipe had her dismount, and they stood in line, waiting their turn. As they inched forward, she eyed those stepping between the arches with trepidation.

"Does portal travel hurt?"

"Not exactly. But neither is it entirely pleasant."

"What do you mean?"

"No one is quite sure how the portals work. Well, Lucifer might, but he's never told anyone. I can say that stepping into one is like dipping your whole body into the coldest thing imaginable."

"Like a cold swim."

"Worse. Because it's not fluid but existence itself. Space. It's like you become a piece of ice that shatters into a thousand pieces and then is put back together on the other side."

"That sounds awful. Is it dangerous?"

"Not usually."

At his less-than-promising words, she shot him a worried glance.

He grinned. "Don't worry. They don't lose too many travelers. It wouldn't be good for business if they did."

Before she could retort, it was their turn, and he was right. It was awful, yet ... somehow oddly familiar. As if she'd been there before, even if she didn't recall it.

In that dark void connecting the rings, she felt her body disintegrate, but her consciousness remained. The numbing cold touched her, but having spent her early years in the dark depths of the Darkling Sea, it didn't bother her. The distant whisper though? Those made her incorporeal form shiver.

Jen-n-n-n-y.

The disembodied voice echoed her name around her, seeking, bouncing the sound around the floating particles of her existence. She wanted to cry out for Felipe, to feel his reassuring hand wrapped around hers, but in this space between worlds, on a plane that held no life, no existence, no substance, she was alone.

Yet not.

Jenny. Jenny. Jenny.

The voice chanted her name, and in that moment, she was glad she didn't have a voice, else she might have made a sound and drawn its attention to her. But even despite her muteness, something *saw* her.

She felt it coming, almost like a rushing wind, sending her motes of self tumbling in a frenzy as it drew nearer and nearer. The icy determination and menace reached out and—

Out she stumbled into the red glare and heat of Hell, the ash gusting in swirls around her face making her blink. She barely had a moment to draw a breath when Felipe was grabbing her and hugging her, practically cracking her ribs.

"What the fuck happened?" he demanded.

"What do you mean?" she asked, still somewhat dazed.

"For a while we thought you were lost. I came out of the portal, but you didn't follow."

"What are you talking about?" she asked, her mind slowly recovering from the odd journey, the cold edge of fear melting in the heat.

"I mean the portal didn't spit you after I came through. At least not right away. You went in over three hours ago."

"Three hours? But it only seemed like minutes…" Her voice trailed off. So she'd not imagined the strange encounter in the dark place. "I don't suppose you heard a voice while going through?"

He frowned at her question. "Through where? The portal? No. Why?"

"Nothing, but I think from now on I'll stick to the longer method of travel overland."

"Probably a good plan given your close call."

Close call or just temporary escape? For some reason Jenny couldn't help but think that whatever searched for her in between the planes was the same thing seeking her out in Hell. Question was, could she stay out of its grasp?

Chapter Nineteen

The fear and anxiety he'd suffered when Jenny didn't emerge from the portal wasn't something Felipe would ever forget. In his anxiety, he'd completely lost his furry mind, going so far as letting his cat loose as he attempted to jump back through and search for her. However, the portal wouldn't allow it. He lunged and jumped, hit the swirling disk, and, much like a bug on a windshield, found himself squashed, face first, slightly stunned at the impact and then sliding in slow motion to hit the ground.

Not one of his more noble moments.

During that three-hour wait, no one could step into the swirling depths of the rip, although Felipe kept testing, going so far as grabbing a passing imp and tossing him at the portal. The bruised fellow cast him many a dark glare as it stomped off, one of his horns bent at an odd angle.

The three hours he spent waiting for a sign or answer were the longest of his life and most nerve-wracking. He'd paced first as a cat in front of it then as a man, cursing aloud at every mage who showed up. One by one they declared themselves baffled. Even the oldest, wisest crone of them all, Nefertiti, couldn't give him a definitive reply as to whether Jenny lived or not.

With her hunched frame but strikingly lively eyes, Nefertiti, whom many claimed lived with a harem made up of hundreds of Hell's handsomest, most virile males, cackled as she said,

"Fear not, kitty. I think your lady friend yet lives. Our Lord has plans for her and you." An ominous declaration, one he didn't have a chance to question because, without warning, Jenny, her lips blue, her skin cold but amazingly enough alive, was spit out by the interdimensional rip.

He caught her in his arms, hugging her tight, the tension within him easing as she appeared unharmed. Yet the fact he'd cared so much in the first place sounded a giant warning bell. His relief was for more than just the fact he'd not failed in his mission. He was happy to see her. Reassured at her wholeness. Feeling a wave of protectiveness, a strong one that urged him to mark her and tie her to him, giving him a tender thread that he could use to track her in the future.

A crazy, impulsive idea, which he was sure would dissipate once the shock of her almost-demise wore off. Sure, he cared for Jenny. She'd become a valued companion and friend. He'd miss her when she was gone. *I don't want her to leave.*

Where did that thought come from?

Keep her.

His cat tossed in its two cents, which prompted Felipe to say to her as he led her away from the now functioning portal and its backlog of people waiting to use it, "If you're willing to ride for an hour, we can arrive at Lucifer's castle before nightfall." Where he could rid himself of Jenny before he did something foolish and permanent.

It didn't take a genius to realize at this point that his brilliant plan to bed her often wasn't working. Not only did his hunger for her grow instead of decrease with each encounter, more and more he dreaded parting from her. He didn't like what it meant.

"You mean that doorway didn't drop us into the first ring?"

He shook his head. No portals were allowed direct travel to the inner ring, Lucifer's paranoia not allowing it. "Might as well give them a fucking key and invite them to invade," was the great Lord's reply when anyone dared to ask. But no one ever complained. Complaints, which Lucifer called whining, often ended up with the whiner in question getting thrown in the stomping vats where, once strained of all bodily fluids, fermented, and bottled, created some fine vintages for the vampires who could afford them.

"The rip took us to the second ring, right on the edge. But from here to the castle we'll have decent roads to travel and even better, guards patrolling them, making the likelihood of attack unlikely."

"That close? I could really use a shower and change of garments," she said with a wrinkle of her nose. Down veered her gaze to her travel-stained clothing, the few hours ride before their trip through the portal having taken its toll, especially when they ran into a flock of hell-ickens. They weren't dangerous, and tasted quite good when basted with butter and garlic. However, their method of defense was less than pleasant. They dropped eggs when frightened, ticking little time bombs that exploded and hit anything in its radius with sulfuric-stinking, slimy yolk.

Her plus water and no clothing? It wasn't just his cat purring at the image. But no, he needed to start putting a distance between them.

"I guess we could stop somewhere for the night, and I could deliver you to the boss in the morning." One more night wouldn't kill him.

"I think I like that plan better. It will be nice to get clean and a last night of sleep before meeting the big man." She tossed him a smile, one he'd come to know all too well.

Apparently a shower wasn't the only thing she had in mind. Problem was Felipe no longer knew if he could trust himself with her. Now that the end of their journey had practically arrived, his cat paced inside his head, protesting and demanding they do something.

I'm not leashing myself to one woman. His statement fell on deaf ears. His feline practically smirked and clearly conveyed a, *I'd like to see you stop me* attitude.

Did he dare allow himself one more night in Jenny's arms? Could he chance losing control for just one second and doing something that would alter the course of his future? Paint his belly yellow. He was afraid to find out.

She frowned at him when they reached the inn and he asked for a room with two beds. As he carried their meager gear up the stone steps, she questioned him. "Since when do we need two beds? Or is this for appearance sake?"

"Listen, Jenny. You're a nice girl and all…"

"I hear the big but coming," she mumbled.

"However, as I told you from the start, I'm not boyfriend material."

"I wasn't asking you to go steady," she snapped as they reached their door. "I'm perfectly aware I'm not the type of girl anyone would want to settle down with. I just thought we would enjoy one more night of fun."

Her words hit him like a slap. He had to bite his tongue not to jump to her defense and tell her it wasn't her who was the problem, but him. She was too wonderful to tie herself down to the likes of him. *Yet Remy, the biggest ladies man around, managed to turn over a new leaf.* Couldn't he? And what if he didn't? He never wanted to hurt Jenny. Because then he'd have to kill himself. A dilemma for sure. One best avoided, no matter how cowardly.

"Yeah, well, I was kind of planning to sit in the bar for a little while. Listen to the gossip and catch up on what's been happening since I left to fetch you."

"Because I was just a job, and the job's done." The tight way she said it shrunk his usually big ego into domestic cat-sized. He didn't like it at all. Just like he didn't enjoy the disappointment in her eyes, the hurt he could sense and the sensation he was being a monumental idiot when he walked away.

But it was for the best, right? Felipe wasn't ready to settle down no matter how much he liked Jenny or how she made him feel. The domestic life wasn't for him, even if he was tired of bouncing from bed to bed, town to town, never knowing where he'd end up or where his next meal would come from. If he failed to appear one day, would anyone notice or care?

Ysabel would. But how long before she sent out an alarm? Felipe was a free spirit, roaming without care or contact sometimes for weeks on end.

However, what would he do otherwise? Pair up with a green-haired temptress and embark on whatever mad scheme Lucifer had planned for her? Stick to her side, protecting her from Undines and other menaces to her safety?

Make love to her each night until he got her with child then expanding his protective circle to a cub?

Ack! He couldn't blame a hairball this time for his choking fit.

Lucky for him, he knew what would soothe his clogged throat. Ale. Lots of it.

Chapter Twenty

After her near-death incident, or whatever it was she'd almost experienced, Jenny could have used some close contact. In other words, she needed to feel Felipe's arms around her, his naked skin touching hers giving her the warmth only he seemed able to impart, to chase away the chill still invading her.

Something dark and deadly wanted her. Why, she couldn't say. Perhaps Lucifer would know. More than likely it was tied into the reason he so keenly wanted her. A pity she couldn't get the one person she truly wanted to feel the same way.

What baffled her was the fact she could have sworn Felipe had grown to care for her. She understood she was naïve when it came to affairs of the heart. She'd not had much personal experience, and yet, she wasn't completely oblivious. She'd caught the way he often stared at her, expression bemused. At other times smoldering. She'd seen his genuine fear and relief when she'd emerged from the rip, and he could argue all he wanted, but she knew in that moment that it wasn't his task for Lucifer and the fear of failure that made him feel that way.

He cared for her. Maybe he didn't quite love her—*not like I fear I've grown to love him*—but he felt something, something more than lust.

She didn't doubt she could seduce him. It wouldn't take much she'd wager, but of course to do that, she kind of needed him present. But he'd chosen to escape instead, to truly drink and catch up on the news, or to hide?

The knock at the door startled Jenny from her thoughts. Had Felipe changed his mind? Decided to indulge in one last night of passion?

Except he wouldn't knock.

So who would? Who knew they were here?

She crept to the door, careful to remain silent. She even held her breath. Pressing her ear against the tarnished wood, she listened.

"We know you are in there, Jenny of Siren Isle," said a female voice. "We've been sent by the Dark Lord to escort you to him."

Apparently, Felipe had changed his mind about them staying the night. So much for presenting herself to Lucifer freshly bathed and mind clear of fatigue. Had Felipe called the moment he'd gone downstairs? It seemed odd.

"How do I know you're telling the truth?"

"We bear the Dark Lord's seal."

Seal? Somehow she doubted they meant the aquatic kind. Keeping the chain on the door latched, Jenny inched the wooden slab open and peered out the gap. "Let me see."

A gold disk was pushed through the slit, its surface corroded and pitted with age, but bearing the unmistakable mien of a man with horns and a devilish smile. It appeared authentic. But then again, Jenny had never seen a seal before, so she couldn't truly judge. She glanced again through the crack to catch a better glimpse of the woman in question. Clad in black combat gear, the soldier stood with three others, all similarly attired. They wore swords strapped to their sides, polished black boots, and chest armor while shaded riot masks hid their features.

Nothing seemed out of place, and yet, Jenny couldn't stop a nagging sense of unease.

"Where is Felipe?"

"Down in the bar with the other half of my squadron."

"I want to see him."

"Why? He's been relieved of his duties now that we are here."

"I should thank him. He's saved my life more than once on our journey. It doesn't seem right to just leave without saying goodbye."

"Very well, but make it quick."

Since Jenny hadn't undressed, it didn't take her long to prepare herself. A quick swirl of her cloak settling around her shoulders and she was ready.

Or not.

Within, a stubborn part of her wanted to argue with Felipe some more. She couldn't believe that after all they shared, he'd not come to care for her a little. What of all his kind gestures? Affectionate caresses? The ferocious care and protectiveness he'd displayed? Surely, it meant something.

I believed him when he said I was special. Trusted him. Was it all a lie?

Unbidden, the old doubts and insecurities fought to rise, to drown her in a mire of depression. But if she'd learned one thing on their voyage, it was that even if she wasn't a pureblood anything, or perfect physically, it didn't mean she had to feel shame. *I am Jenny, and I am worth something.* To the Dark Lord at least, who was concerned enough for welfare, he'd sent numerous guards to escort her to the safety—she hoped—of his castle.

Felipe or not, someone wanted her. Chin tilted and jaw set, she flung open the door, startling the black-clad group, whose leather armor creaked as they formed a semicircle before her.

"Let's go."

With the one she'd spoken to leading the way, they headed down the hall and clattered down the rickety steps into the bar proper.

It wasn't hard to spot Felipe even amidst the patron filled tavern. He was the one with voluptuous woman on his lap, her platinum, curled locks falling around her almost-bare shoulders.

Ire battled hurt. Jealousy had Jenny clenching her fists so tight her nails cut crescents into her palms.

"There's the cat. Didn't take him long to find a new toy to play with. Still want to say goodbye?" asked the leader mockingly. "If you ask me, he seems a tad … *busy*."

"Fuck him." The foul words spat from her mouth. To think she'd lamented over him upstairs. About to whirl and give him her back, she instead stumbled, barely catching herself as the female straddling him was sent to the floor in a squealing heap.

It was no accident. Felipe rose to his full height, the lines in his body betraying his anger. Jenny realized why a moment later. The blonde, who wasn't a true blonde after all, had lost her wig in the scuffle. It hit the floor, revealing tightly pinned, dark green dreads. The coiled strands of a mermaid who'd thought to accost him undercover.

And she wasn't alone. Cloaked figures in the room threw back their hoods to reveal their seaweed tresses. Jenny's hand went to her amulet, the one nullifying her deadly voice. But before she tore it off, she glanced over her shoulder at Lucifer's guard to warn them. "We're being attacked by mermaids. We need to help him."

"To a watery grave. Or given the lack of an ocean, at least a bloody one," was the leader's reply. To Jenny's horror, she tore off her helmet, revealing her true identity. *I was duped.*

Yanking at the thong holding the amulet, Jenny fought to unleash her deadly song, but before she could utter a note, something conked her on the back of the head—*not again!*—and everything went black.

Chapter Twenty-one

Drowning his sorrows in ale seemed like the best idea after Felipe left Jenny. Problem was Felipe didn't think there was enough alcohol to make him forget that, in just a few hours, he'd find himself parted from her.

Which, as I told her, is for the best.

He wasn't ready to settle down. Or was he? It hadn't escaped his notice that since he'd met his enchanting half-mermaid, he'd not given another look or thought to another woman. The sirens, despite their beauty, did not attract him. The Amazons, with their openness about sex and their less-than-subtle offers to bed him, he'd ignored or outright refused. Hell, even the buxom blonde sashaying her way toward him with full lips and rounded hips stirred nothing in him other than annoyance. Did she not know he preferred his women with greenish-blonde curls, an impish smile, and a husky voice only he could tolerate?

Don't they know Jenny's the one?

Of course they didn't because even he refused to accept it. His cat even now yowled in his head, a wordless noise that basically said, *You're a fucking idiot. Go and claim her.*

Did the what-if's really matter? If a womanizing demon like Remy could settle down with one woman and be happy, couldn't he? If the devil could restrict himself to sex with one woman, wasn't he capable? He could at least try instead of being such a fraidy cat, especially since yellow wasn't his color.

He went through the reasons why he shouldn't. What did he have to offer her? A small apartment? A dangerous job that saw him traveling for the Dark Lord? Petty excuses because he knew those were things Jenny didn't give a flying fuck about.

He'd seen how her face lit up on their journey. After her exile on the isle, she'd probably appreciate getting out to explore the rings of Hell and the fucked-up wonders within. As for his living accommodations, he could always get a bigger place. They both could. *Damn, we could share rent and an apartment.* Imagine waking up beside her every day. To gaze into those stormy blue eyes every morning. To kiss and touch—

His reverie was rudely interrupted as a heavily perfumed body plopped itself in his lap. "Hello there, stranger," hummed a low female voice. "What brings you here?"

"Sorry, darling, you'll have to ply your wares elsewhere. I'm a taken man." Look at that. Saying it aloud didn't cause Hell to freeze over. On the contrary, the pit now appeared brighter to him than a moment ago. The depression within him eased.

What was he doing sitting here being an idiot when he had a ready-and-willing lover waiting upstairs?

"We're in Hell. Cheating is expected and encouraged," she said with a lick of her lips. She draped her arms around his neck, bringing her prodigious bosom almost eye level, but it left Felipe cold. She wasn't Jenny, and for that matter, he could just imagine the jealous fit Jenny would throw if she caught him with this hussy on his lap.

Good thing he'd told her to stay in the room. A room he'd shortly join her in.

"What part of not interested did you not grasp?" was his curt reply. His nose twitched, the heavy perfume bothering it, but it was more than that. He could scent a subtle undertone. A hint of—brine?

Cold clarity made him eye more keenly the less-than-subtle whore still draping him. A woman with extremely pale skin, bearing an almost green pallor. "Bloody mermaid." He muttered it like a curse as he shoved her from his lap to the floor, knocking off in the process the blonde wig she wore to cover her true seaweed hair.

But where there was one mermaid…

It didn't take the howl of his cat to realize that many of the cloaked figures in the room were the enemy. The flinging back of numerous hoods and the draw of weapons did that quite adequately.

However, it was the hint of movement beyond their menacing approach that drew his eye. Drew it, held it, and enraged the beast within. Jenny stood at the bottom of the stairs, one hand clutched to her neck, surrounded by dark armored troops, only they weren't the Dark Lord's guard because none of them would have torn off a mask to reveal their mermaid tresses while another used the hilt of her sword to bash his sweet Jenny on the skull.

Fuck.

This wasn't good. Time to unleash his kitty.

With a mighty roar, his other shape burst free, shredding the clothes he wore. Fur bristling, teeth slavering, and his eyes promising some serious injury, he lunged in the direction of those holding Jenny and dragging her to the door. However, bodies got in his way, prey who thought to keep him from his mate.

With a snarl, he tore into them, and blood flowed. However, it wasn't just the essence of his enemy that painted the inn's floor but his own as the aquatic females drew their blades to hack at him. He did his best to dodge and eliminate the threats. Each step he managed to take forward cost him, though, in strength and injury. He drew upon all his skill as a hunter and fighter to stay alive, to reach Jenny to save her, to—

He blinked his eyes open and stared at the frescoed ceiling. The images of woodland nymphs cavorting made for an interesting, if disturbing, view. Disturbing because he had no recollection of ever seeing them before.

How did I get here? And where is here? The last thing he recalled…

"Fuck!" As memories of the battle unfolded, including his sudden blackout, he sprang to his feet on the soft bed he found himself in, naked and, as he noted in that same instant, uninjured. Hands slapping at his flesh, he noted new scars, healed ones. He did a quick mental check and growled as he noted he'd lost a life. That didn't leave him with many. Damn those mermaids.

"I see you're finally awake."

The feminine voice came from beyond the filmy curtains hiding the bed. Batting them aside, he hopped to the stone floor and faced his boss's girlfriend, Mother Earth.

"Goodness, I see now why you're so popular with the ladies." Gaia's gaze perused him from head to toe, a smile curving her lips.

Not good because her interest was sure to put a scowl on Lucifer's face and probably end up with him spending a few centuries paying for it. The sin of jealousy was one the Dark Lord particularly enjoyed. "I don't suppose I could have some privacy, ma'am."

"How about a pair of pants instead," she compromised, snapping her fingers.

Felipe didn't yelp as fabric suddenly covered his man parts, but it was close. "Thank you, my lady." He sketched a quick bow.

"No need for such formalities. You may call me Gaia."

Yeah, no. He'd prefer to keep his limbs. "Where am I, and what happened? Last thing I remember, I was fighting mermaids in the bar."

"Yes, and you acquitted yourself quite well, especially given the number thrown against you. Alas, it wasn't enough, and by the time the guard arrived, you'd spent a life, and Jenny was gone."

"Gone?" Cold dread formed a pit in his stomach.

"Kidnapped by those cold-blooded fish and taken to the Styx, where they dove into the waves. We lost track of her at that point."

"We?"

"Yes. My Lord and I have been tracking your progress. Or at least I was. Lucifer was otherwise occupied last night, else the skirmish might have ended quite differently. As to where you are, given the gravity of your injuries, I removed you to my castle where I could tend to you."

"How long have I been here?"

"Time flows differently here. Suffice it to say, you've been here a while, but you'll return in time."

"Time for what?"

"To rescue her of course. You do plan to get her back?"

No hesitation. "Well duh. If I don't, Lucifer will string me up and rip out my entrails."

"And is that the only reason you want to find her?"

For a moment, Felipe almost lied. However, caught by the swirling green gaze of Mother Earth, he couldn't. "No. Even if he ordered me to forget Jenny, I would still go to her rescue."

Apparently, that was the correct answer because a smile bloomed across Gaia's face, a blinding one. If it weren't for his affection for a certain lady, he might have fallen prisoner to its captivating spell. "I see my Lord was right once again in his pairing. Who knew he had such a knack?"

Words that made no sense to Felipe, but Gaia didn't bother to explain.

She clapped her hands. "Well then, if we are to mount an effective rescue, you must make haste. The mermaids and their prize are hours ahead of you at the moment."

"I thought time had no meaning."

"No, it still passes, just not at the same rate. When I return you, only a few hours shall have passed."

"So, they don't have much of a head start, but the bigger dilemma is how to catch them. According to your spies, they entered the Styx, which places them underwater. I want to save her, but how?" The hopelessness of the task hit him like a well-aimed imp tossed in a game of Dodgeskull. If the mermaids had taken her to the Darkling Sea, how would he find her, let alone rescue her?

"What's with the sad face?"

"The task is impossible."

"Is it? Have you so little faith in your Lord and his abilities? Lucifer will give you the tools needed to help you in your quest."

"If he doesn't kill me for failing in the first place," he muttered. But if it took facing the wrath of his boss to save the woman he loved— and by all his whiskers he did love Jenny—then off to the castle he'd go. He still had a few lives to spare.

Chapter Twenty-two

Striking a pose, Lucifer eyed his latest outfit in the mirror with a critical eye. He was still torn as to what to wear.

Pirate apparel replete with billowy white shirt adorned with hanging ruffled sleeves, breeches, a faux peg leg and eye patch? Colonial commander with heavy brocade jacket, large tricorn hat and powdered curls? Navy style with full admiral gear and a full array of medals—awards he'd given himself over the centuries for valor and other brave acts?

Or should he go completely badass and dress in black, which had a slimming effect and meant he could wear his cool black cape and tungsten-toed black Hessian boots?

Decisions. Decisions. Half the battle was making a daunting impression on the enemy. Then crushing them. And once crushed, he needed to look his best for the reporters sure to swarm him after.

His hellphone rang, the tone a special one titled "The Cat Came Back," done by a cool jazz group who played in a disreputable club in the seventh ring.

About time Felipe reported in. He'd wondered when the damnable feline would call. The overland travel when the portal in the Amazon village malfunctioned—a problem he'd secretly manufactured to give his latest dating duo more time to spend together—had delayed the arrival of his new minion. Problem was he'd had a difficult time tracking them in between the towns they pit-stopped in. His spy network apparently needed a major overhaul. He knew they'd finally made it to the second ring, not that he let on he knew. Let the minions think they could act as they wanted and he was more likely to catch them misbehaving.

"If it isn't my mangy feline finally deigning to report in. Where in the nine rings are you?" he barked.

"Right outside the bloody castle where your fucking guard is refusing me entry."

"Of course they are. It's what I pay them to do. No entry to anyone without my say-so. We are in lock-down mode." A precaution given the portents his seers kept bitching about. End of Hell as we know it, blah, blah. They screamed death and destruction. Lucifer called it about time he had some fun.

"Problems in the capital, boss?"

"Not yet, but my horns are humming, which means it's coming. A demon can never be too prepared. I will relay orders for my guards to allow you in along with the girl."

Felipe cleared his throat. "Uh. Yeah, about that. We have a slight problem."

"What do you mean a slight problem?"

"I don't have Jenny anymore."

"What do you mean you don't have her anymore? My spies said you hit the edge of the second ring last night and booked into a tavern with lodgings."

"Didn't your spies tell you what happened next?"

Probably, but Lucifer hadn't read the reports yet. He'd spent a busy evening chasing

Mother Nature around his garden and then deflowering her. She'd left him not long after, citing pressing business, and he'd spent the rest of the night catching up on the latest episodes of *Game of Thrones*. Now there was a bloody show with a cast he could admire.

"I don't have time to watch over every single foolish minion. I'm a busy man. So get on with it, cat. Tell me how you fucked up."

"I got taken by surprise by mermaids. They showed up in disguise, and while I did my best to fight them off, there were too many. They took Jenny."

"You lost your mission objective." Lucifer's voice dropped into a low, ominous growl.

"She was taken, no thanks to your fucking damned souls and lazy demons who watched the whole thing happen without lifting a finger. Not to mention, how did the mermaids make it past so many of your guards in the first place?"

"Are you making excuses? Trying to shift blame? Not taking responsibility? All admirable sins, but don't think you can placate me with your refusal to take responsibility."

"How about I atone by promising to get her back."

"You know where she is?"

"Not quite, but I can guess."

And so could Lucifer. He eyed his nautical outfits and saw his mind had already peeked ahead to the future. "Meet me at the docks."

He hung up his phone and sent out a few directives with just a snap of his fingers. As people jumped to do his bidding, he dressed until there was only one thing left to do.

"Gaia!" He bellowed her name. This time she didn't make him wait but arrived in a rose-perfumed cloud.

"You bellowed, my randy lover?"

"How would you like to go on a fishing cruise?" he asked.

It was time for this demon to become king of the Darkling Sea and show certain fishies what happened to those who attacked on his turf and took what he considered his.

Chapter Twenty-three

Nerves stretched taut and his kitty snapping and snarling in his head, Felipe paced the ancient stone dock jutting from the first circle into the Styx.

Not so long ago, he'd stood in this very same spot, a feline getting its paw slapped by his boss. He'd returned a different man. Now, instead of looking for an excuse to flee Lucifer's machinations, he wanted to be a part of them. He needed his Lord's help in going to the rescue of the one person who'd come to mean more to him than even his own lives; someone he loved. *Ack.* Damned hairballs.

Choking on the admission or not, it was time for him to embrace the truth. He loved Jenny, and if it meant readjusting some of his views and practicing monogamy and coming home to the same place and woman every night, he would because he'd found something worth the collar and leash. A woman who engaged him on all levels—and made him fucking purr.

Despite tardiness being a sin, Felipe didn't have to wait for long. His Lord stepped from a temporary portal onto the dock, dressed in black combat gear from head to toe, which would have proven much more impressive if not for the yellow rain slicker he wore overtop.

At Felipe's arched brow, Lucifer said, "It takes a confident demon to pull this off. I thought the rubber duckies added a playful touch."

Playful or insane? Not a debate he'd verbalize given Felipe preferred to keep his head.

"So how are we getting to Jenny, boss? Military sub? Special forces scuba team? Going to part the waters and choke the bitches? Take a direct portal to their hideout and wipe them out with your army?"

"We are going by boat, of course. Damned portals won't work over water."

"Boat?" Felipe was about to ask what boat since there was nothing anchored when, from the mists of the Styx, appeared a familiar shape. A robed Charon poled his flatbed vessel to the dock.

A smart kitty would have held his tongue. Apparently, he'd lost some of his intelligence with his last life. "You aren't fucking serious, are you? We'll never catch them in that rickety old thing."

"Rickety?" Charon drew himself to his full height, which was remarkably impressive. "I'll have you know this vessel is extremely reliable. I've ferried millions of souls with it. Fought off beasts. Engaged in battles."

"Took the animals two by two," Felipe added sarcastically. "We get it. The thing's a relic."

"Shut it," Lucifer commanded, stepping onto the deck. "If you want to save your lady and your skin, I suggest you get your furry ass on board." Lucifer took a place in the prow and tucked his hands behind his back.

Trusting his boss had a plan, Felipe followed, resisting an urge to body check Charon, who oozed smugness and amusement.

Using his long pole for propulsion, Charon pushed off, the only sound the slapping of the water against the dock. No fanfare. No announcement. No media. How strange. Lucifer was usually more of the grandstanding type.

Gray mist encircled them almost immediately, a pea soup that didn't allow for any visibility. Felipe didn't like it at all, the moisture clinging to his skin especially irritating his inner feline, which couldn't help but remind him that the last time they'd trusted a vessel to take them on water they'd ended up in the drink.

He didn't let his fear send him swimming back to shore. Jenny needed him. Thankfully, they didn't have to go too far.

Charon muttered, "We're here," and rapped his pole against the side of a large shape which suddenly appeared on their starboard side. A reply came from the fog, the low trumpeting of a horn. As if a signal, the heavy mist parted, and Felipe stared up, then up some more at the gigantic metal monster floating on the Styx.

This is more like it!

The massive military ship, outfitted with a machine gun turret, old style cannons, several harpoons and more, was painted a flat black, except for the prow where red flames zigzagged from bloodshot eyeballs. Its name? The *S.S. SushiMaker.*

"Big enough for you, cat?" Lucifer asked, flinging his yellow slicker over one shoulder as they came alongside.

"It'll do," was his nonchalant reply. He scrambled up the ladder after his boss, who, despite his age, proved more agile than expected.

Swinging himself onto the deck, Felipe did a double take at the robed figure already waiting there. "How did—" Felipe halted himself as he stared down at the empty waves slapping against the ship. Welcome to Hell, where strange shit happened.

And fashion sense was skewed. In the seconds it took Felipe to realize Charon was indeed on deck before him, he'd acquired an admiral's cap, black of course, with gold braid across it. It should have looked odd sitting on Charon's head given he still wore his hooded robe—which now bore admiral's stripes on the sleeves—and yet, it didn't.

With a floating gait—did the guy not have feet?—Charon led Felipe and their boss to the upper deck into the command center. Demons manned the controls, a distant thump and hum making the whole vessel rumble. Hell's navy about to go kick some mermaid ass.

"Hold on tight, kitty," Lucifer advised, "because this suped-up warship is about to go seriously nautical."

Felipe would have laughed, except the ship lurched, threw him off balance, and then he was scrambling to find something to hold on to as the *S.S. SushiMaker* didn't just ride the waves, it sliced them, diced them, and moved at a ridiculous speed.

When he did finally gather a breath, he shouted, "What kind of engine does this thing have?"

"Engine? You know that shit can't be relied on in Hell. This sucker is powered old school, with oars," Lucifer boasted. He tapped at a button, and the sonar screen flashed to a scene below deck.

Gaping, Felipe stared at the hundreds of rowers, a good number of them Vikings. And happy as shit. The sound he'd taken for an engine hum? The rowers chanting while a drummer kept the beat.

"*Row, row, row the boat, toward the Darkling Sea.*

And there we'll find some fucking fish, and have a killing spree."

Each time they sang a verse, they cheered. A berserker army on its way to glory.

Felipe began to feel a little more optimistic, especially since he doubted the mermaids had access to such speed. Perhaps there was hope they'd catch them in time. In time for what though, no one seemed to know.

Chapter Twenty-four

The mermaids came prepared, which in one respect boded well for Jenny since they needed her alive. When she regained consciousness in the murky water, it was to find a mouthpiece taped to her jaw, feeding her oxygen. On the other hand, though, not dying quickly probably meant they wanted something from her. Given they weren't exactly gentle in their handling of her as they dragged her underwater, their powerful tails propelling them, it meant they just needed her alive long enough to reach their destination and then…

That was what she didn't know. Why did the mermaids want her so bad? Why did Lucifer? *Let's not also forget that scary entity in the portal. And how come the one person I want to want me is the only one willing to let me go?*

Given a choice between dwelling on her depressing forced breakup with Felipe and her probable impending death, she chose neither. Her siren aunts hadn't raised her to mope around and lament her fate. Strong women decided their fate. Just because she couldn't charm the pants off anything with a penis didn't mean she didn't have other skills. But how to sing her way to freedom when she not only wore the amulet still but her hands were bound and her mouth taped to a regulator?

She'd have to find a way. Given her captors didn't pay her much attention, only occasionally adjusting their grip on her hair, which they used to painfully tow her, Jenny tried to work on the knots binding her wrists.

Hours later, she'd almost managed to get the final knot undone when someone finally noticed. Or so she assumed when she awoke to another throbbing headache and her hands once again firmly tied. *Argh!*

On a positive note, she wasn't in the water anymore and her mouth was free. Licking her lips, she peered around, the light dim but not so much that she didn't recognize the spot. Her shoulders slumped.

Welcome home.

Kind of. She found herself in her old living quarters. Well, cave. A ten-by-ten cell with a moldy pallet and a few broken toys covered in a layer of lichen from disuse. It seemed the place she'd called home for the first few years of her life hadn't hosted any new occupants or a cleaning as the scratchings on the walls, pictures she'd drawn, still decorated it.

How Jenny had loved the crayons smuggled to her, a present from an anonymous donor. She'd used their brightness to adorn her cell with pictures she'd seen in the few books she'd owned. Childish renderings of sunshine and trees. Stick figures and flowers. A sad attempt by a child, punished for her birth, to bring color to her life.

A life she wasn't ready to give up, no matter how dire the situation.

Struggling to her feet, Jenny staggered to the wall and found a ragged stone edge. She sawed at her tethers, ignoring the pain as she occasionally abraded her skin in her haste. She'd have worse things to worry about than a few drops of her blood if she didn't escape.

When the last tendril snapped, she wasted no time ripping the amulet from around her neck and stuffing it in a pocket of her toga. Let the mermaids come. She'd greet them with a song.

Crouching by the wall, she took up watch, eying the lapping edge of the sea against the floor of her cave, not letting her mind wander. She couldn't afford to. *I need to save myself.* No whiskered kitty would come bounding to her rescue. No singing blonde sirens would yodel her abductors into submission.

She was well and truly alone. But not defeated.

Without a window to the outside, she couldn't gauge the passage of time, but she would have guessed a few hours passed before Mommy Dearest finally dared to pop in her seaweed-covered head. From the ripples in the water, Mother rose, her eyes unblinking, her lips unsmiling.

Jenny met her cold gaze with an even icier grin. "Hello, Mother." Then she sang a little ditty, "Step on a crack, break the bitch's back. Sing a happy spiel and merrily she'll keel."

She should have known the woman who'd birthed her and hated her would have protection from her voice. Still, it had been worth a try.

Rising from the water until only her tail remained submerged, her mother's lidless black orbs perused her. "Just as deformed as ever I see. I should have let you drown at birth."

Imagine that, her mother was still as hateful as ever. "Why didn't you? You've always despised me."

"Yes. You're an abomination. You should have never been born, especially of my body," she hissed.

"Any guess as to who's not getting a nomination for mother of the year?" Jenny muttered.

Hatred made her mother ugly as she spat, "I might have birthed you, but I am not your mother. You are no child of mine, abomination. Merely something I had to suffer."

"So why didn't you give me away at birth? I'm sure you could have foisted me upon some fisherman's family. Instead, you kept me here. A prisoner."

"I was given no choice because of the prophecy."

Okay, that wasn't expected. "What are you talking about?"

Colorless lips curved into a smirk. "You didn't think I let you live because I wanted to, did you? I wanted you to die. But you were needed. Or, should I say, your voice was."

"For what?"

"Why, to awaken and free the one who was unjustly imprisoned."

"What are you talking about?"

"You don't need to know. Just sing when you are told."

Hold on a second. The mermaids wanted her to sing? Because of a prophecy? That couldn't bode well. "I'm not doing anything for you."

"You will." Her mother, who refused to acknowledge her even now, made a gesture, and from the water, mermaids rose, four of them, along with four Undines.

Jenny sucked in a breath and sang a few notes, to no effect.

Her mother laughed. "Oh please. We might have misjudged your voice during our early attempts, but we know better now. These worthy volunteers won't fall victim to your mutant power."

Indeed they wouldn't. It horrified Jenny to see the scars where once they'd born ears. The crazy fanatics had rendered themselves deaf in order to escape her power.

Her sense of dread deepened, especially as they pinned her and taped another regulator to her mouth before dragging her into the cold Darkling Sea.

They didn't have far to go. Ringed by a coral reef, carved over time into an amphitheater, the large ceremonial clearing was where rituals were performed and where they dumped her.

Swimming away wasn't an option, not with the dozens of mermaids swimming circles around the sacred spot, not to mention the air bubble they encased her in was tethered to the sea floor. But then again, once Jenny saw who else shared the space, she couldn't have moved anywhere.

In good news, Aunt Molpe had survived the storm that had capsized their boat. The bad news? The mermaids had her.

And when the choice was given, *"Sing or the siren dies,"* Jenny didn't hesitate. She opened her mouth and sang.

Chapter Twenty-five

The brisk and briny air felt good against his face. How long since Lucifer sailed the Darkling Sea? He really needed to take more time to enjoy himself. Working too hard, while sinful because it forced him to neglect other matters, was at the same time a good deed as it showed his dedication. Blech. He couldn't have it said that the great lord couldn't slack off with the best of them.

His feline minion paced the deck, so worried and in love it made Lucifer both happy and nauseous. On the one hand—six-fingered, which came in handy when strumming his girlfriend—his plan to pair the cat with Jenny worked. *Fist pump to Hell's greatest matchmaker.* But on the other hand—four fingered and tipped with claws more deadly than a certain mutant—what was it about love that turned perfectly disreputable men into pussies?

Thank fuck I haven't fallen victim to that emasculating emotion. Sure, he liked Gaia, but you didn't see him changing himself into someone else. Okay, so he didn't screw around anymore or visit the titty bars, and he'd toned down his belching at the dinner table and no longer came to bed wearing the blood of his enemies, but he did those things for sex. Not out of affection. And anyone who dared say otherwise would make a great lampshade for his office.

"Lord Lucifer! Giant clam, starboard." For a moment, he visualized a hairy clam between creamy thighs. Ah for the seventies before shaving became the norm.

But wait, the lookout meant an actual shellfish. Starboard? Which fucking side was that? Probably the one where a white ribbed shell bobbed on the waves. Strange because didn't those things usually sit on the bottom of the ocean?

"Demons to the harpoons. Goblins to the cannons. If I give the order, turn that overgrown mollusk into pink slime." He'd never been a chowder kind of guy. Shrimp, on the other hand, he gorged by the bucket.

With his yellow slicker protecting him from the spray coming off the waves—and ensuring his visibility to those who heeded his orders—Lucifer strode closer, one hand on the hilt of his great sword—his forged one, not his mighty fleshy one.

The seashell inched open, and he held his hand in the air, holding all fire as he waited to see who or what would emerge. Giant pearl? Enemy crab? That Venus chick, who would so get her ass spanked if she popped out while Gaia was here. Mother Nature wasn't too understanding when his ex-girlfriends came around.

What the mollusk revealed wasn't on his list, and his eyes widened in surprise.

"Well, I'll damn myself, Muriel, what in the nine fucking circles are you doing here? I thought you were on vacation with your harem of men and your daughter?"

Stepping forth from the shell, alone, which was rare, was his daughter by Gaia. Muriel shrugged as she took his hand and hopped onto his deck.

"Yeah, well, you know how it is. My beachside holiday turned into a clusterfuck. New lover. New threat to Hell. Story of my life. So once again, I'm here to save the day and your hairy ass."

"I'll have you know I had it waxed earlier this week."

Muriel wasn't the only one to groan at this revelation. "Too much info. Anyhow— Hold on a second, is that a ducky with horns on your slicker?"

Thrusting his shoulders back, Lucifer grinned as he showed off. "Yes. Do you like it?"

"Only you could hope to carry it off," was her reply. "And is that Gaia standing on the prow of the ship with her arms spread wide? What is she doing?"

"Don't ask. Someone has watched *Titanic* one too many times. But forget about Gaia and her obsession with a certain movie. What are you doing here on my boat?"

"We've got a problem. It seems some big bad entity, who was locked away like eons ago, wants back into our plane of existence."

Another attack by some faceless entity? Awesome, so long as it wasn't another broad. Lucifer was an old-school chauvinist. Was it too much to ask that some power-hungry males come after him for once? "Well, too fucking bad. Whoever it is will have to find another dimension to crash in because I'm not letting it cross over."

"You might not want to, but I don't know if you'll have a choice. Apparently there's a key to unlocking the doorway between our world and whatever plane of existence this psycho power is on. The good news is we can destroy the key. It took us—"

"Us? Us as in who?"

An irritated sigh blew past Muriel's lips. "My newest addition to the family. You'll meet him later. Anyhow, it took us a little while to figure it out, but apparently there's a chick who can cast a spell to open some mega doorway that will call this thing and let it in."

"Who is she? We'll rip her vocal cords out before she can shout 'Boo!'"

"According to all indications, in other words some fish guts spread on some weird psychic's beach, she's somewhere around here. Maybe you've seen or heard of her. Name's Jenny. Apparently she's got a killer voice."

Cue the dramatic music. Lucifer should have known the mission would get interesting. Muriel's arrival had drawn an audience, and one in particular perked his ears at the mention of a certain name.

"Jenny is who we've come to rescue," Felipe announced.

Muriel shook her head. "Forget rescue. She needs to get taken out before the mermaids use her to let the big bad in."

Fists bunched at his side, Felipe growled. "You mean kill her? Like fuck."

Even Lucifer frowned. "I kind of agree with the cat here. Surely there's a better way. I've got my own prophecy, and it says she's going to help in the battle that's coming." As well as give him killer baby minions for his army.

"A battle we can avoid if she's dead before she starts it."

And ruin the only fun he'd had in a while? Women! Always trying to stop wars instead of letting a demon have some bloody fun.

"I won't allow it." Felipe positioned himself in front of Muriel, every line in his body promising aggression.

Uh-oh. Bad idea. Only fools defied his headstrong daughter. Good thing he wore his slicker. Blood might soon splatter.

Muriel fixed Felipe with a hard stare, something she'd gotten better at as life kept tossing her calamities and she fought back, each time emerging stronger and stronger. "Excuse me, but who in Hell are you?"

"I think the better question is who the fuck do you think you are?"

Had Lucifer forgotten to make introductions? Excellent. It seemed he hadn't lost his bad manners.

Indignant, his daughter huffed, "That's it. I'm calling the PR department. As Lucifer's daughter, I demand more respect!"

His daughter might have looked more intimidating if she'd dressed for the part. However, wearing a skimpy bikini, flip-flops, and with tangled surfer-girl hair, his daughter appeared more ready for a swim model photo shoot than ass kicking.

"I don't care who your daddy is, *princess*. You're not killing Jenny."

"And who's going to stop me?" she asked with a smirk.

"I will."

Before anyone could fathom what Felipe meant, he took off running, his form morphing into his Hell kitty, sending his clothes scattering.

When he hit the side of the ship, he perched on the rail, a giant feline about to sacrifice another life. Or not. He seemed to hesitate, probably as he realized there was nowhere to really go. Felipe cocked his head, as if listening to an invisible voice—also known as Lucifer's meddlesome girlfriend—before he launched himself into the swirling whirlpool forming alongside the ship.

Whirlpool? Uh-oh, that didn't bode well, but it tied with what else Lucifer saw emerging from the frothy waves.

His daughter, less concerned about the oceanic catastrophe happening and more about the insult to her person, let out a screech. "I am so going to skin that cat and use him as a rug when I get my hands on him."

"Mind rerouting that murderous impulse to something a little more pressing?" Lucifer asked.

Eyes glowing, as a spark from the fires of Hades lit them from within—a chip off the old block—she faced him and snarled. "What could be more important than making sure your minions respect me?"

Usually Lucifer would have sided with her desire to kill someone for respect, even given her a knife. However, the lookout shouted a damned good reason why everyone needed to focus on the bigger dilemma emerging. "Krakens!"

Chapter Twenty-six

As plans went, this probably ranked as the dumbest. Felipe heard the broad—who was apparently related to his boss—claim they needed to kill Jenny, and Felipe lost his furry mind. It was the only explanation for why he dove into the whirling maelstrom forming in the sea.

Why he chose that spot he couldn't have quite said. Instinct drew him—oh, and the whisper from Gaia and ghostly shove saying, "Go, she's down there. Only you can help her now." How Mother Nature accomplished that when she stood at the prow arms outstretched, laughing in the wind and sea spray he didn't care to wonder about, not when he was caught in an epic swirly.

Around and around he spun, soaked and yet miraculously not drowning, even if he was plenty dizzy. A funnel formed, leading him down. Much like a bobbing piece of flotsam, he let the current take him. He didn't bother to fight the suctioning whirlpool. He saved his strength because it soon became evident it was taking him where he needed to be—the bottom of the ocean where a water-free clearing formed a sandy-based amphitheater. Standing alone and bedraggled in the center, Jenny sang. Tone-deaf or not, it didn't take a music connoisseur to recognize the magic forming.

Whether this Muriel chick liked it or not, and good or bad for Hell, whatever she feared had already begun, and Felipe chose his side.

There was never any question actually. He chose Jenny.

In spite of the roaring water, the distant sound of cannon fire, and even the screams, Felipe couldn't help but hear as Jenny's voice weaved a spell. A mighty one. A terrible one. And yet, the most captivating sound he'd ever heard. Even he could appreciate the haunting beauty of each powerful note. He could practically see them float past him, colorful swirls of esoteric force pulled up the vortex of the whirlpool to a grey sky full of whirling clouds.

When he hit the sandy bottom, littered with the twitching sea life left behind, he lay there gasping for air, trying to regain his wits. However, much like a king cobra, the music held him in thrall, as did the woman uttering the notes.

In the center of the whirlpool's eye, Jenny stood, hair whipping around, the tendrils dancing as if alive. Her toga, a shredded rag barely covering her flesh, fluttered, offering teasing glimpses of her flesh. In her eyes, the wild blue waves danced, and from her mouth, the terrible, beautiful melody poured, growing in sound, expanding in volume. The spell reached its peak.

He staggered to his four furry feet. A part of him recognized he should stop the music. But he didn't need to kill her to do so, just silence her before she could finish. As he went to move in her direction, arms reached from the wall of water ringing the space and grasped at him.

The scrabbling fingers missed. Whirling, he noted the milling school of mermaids, their seaweed hair trailing around them as they thrashed back and forth in the water, their black orbs challenging him to enter their oceanic domain. As if. He snarled at them, inviting them instead to meet him on solid ground, yet none dared cross the watery threshold. He batted at their feeble flails and, when he realized they posed no threat, turned to face Jenny.

Except an obstacle stood in his way. It seemed not all the mermaids feared meeting him. One stood with her seaweed hair streaming down her back, her lips peeled back over gums revealing a vicious snarl. Forget the cute cartoons of mermaids. This aquatic hybrid was the stuff monster legends were made of, and she apparently wanted to kill him.

It wasn't just the long knife she stabbed his way but the uttered, "Die, feline spawn!" that tipped him off. He dodged her first lunge and swiped at her leg, his claws leaving bloody furrows in her skin.

It didn't slow her down. With a scream of rage, she came at him again. However, in her mad dash, she left herself open, and he took full advantage, his teeth ripping through flesh and tearing a major artery. Down to the sand, she slumped, limbs twitching but still spouting vitriol.

"You are too late to stop the abomination. At last my shame will be my triumph. My body and soul will be cleansed of the foul thing done to it."

Too late? Shit. Felipe ignored the dying mermaid to refocus on Jenny and maybe still manage to stop the song.

But he was too late.

Everyone was too late.

The last note rang with a clarity that raised every hair on his body. Up rose the last clarion treble of the spell, a mote of light so stark against the dark sky. It hit the swirling clouds and flashed, leaving in its spot a hole, no, make that a portal, a portal that widened and widened…

Would no one stop it? Jenny had fallen to her knees, panting. Felipe did not have the skills to close it. But what of the others, those who rode the waves?

At the lip of the whirlpool, so far above his head, Felipe could see Lucifer's battleship, a tiny toy tossed and rocked not only by the tempestuous sea but by tentacles. Big tentacles. Holy fuck, were those kraken attacking the ship?

Even at a distance, he could see the zaps of power as the magic users on board shot at their foes. Specks of bodies leapt from the vessel and drove matchsticks into the limbs, the Viking berserkers having a grand old time. However, while everyone was engaged with the danger at hand, no one was paying attention to the massive hole in the sky. And something approached. Something big. Bad. Powerful.

He held his breath. The whole realm probably did. Time seemed almost to stop for a moment, or at least slow down, for he could see everything with such clarity. The ugly rip in the sky, the ringing storm clouds, the blinding flash of light.

He blinked, just for a second, and when he opened his eyes again, the hole in the sky was gone. Vanished without a cloud to be seen. Not a monster in sight. Nothing except the lingering sense the world had changed, but in a way he could not immediately perceive.

His fur stood on end as if electrified. When a hand brushed it down, he whirled with a snarl and snapping jaws.

Jenny snatched back her hand. He immediately calmed down and changed shapes. He crushed her to him. "Thank all the souls in Hell you're safe," he murmured against the top of her head.

"You came for me," she whispered against the bare skin of his chest.

"I will always come for you."

"But you hate the water. You said you'd never sail again."

"Yeah, well, love makes a man do stupid things."

She froze in his arms. "What did you say?"

Too much. "So, I hear your singing is supposed to bring about some kind of apocalypse."

The twitch of her lips was probably a smile against his chest as he less than deftly changed the subject. "I wasn't given much choice. They had my aunt. It was either sing as the mermaids ordered, or they would have killed her. I would rather die than see any of my aunts come to harm."

"You know Lucifer hates altruism."

"You think he'll be mad?"

"Nah. Because, lucky for you, he loves a good war. If you ask me, he wanted this to happen."

"What makes you say that?"

"Just a funny feeling."

She tilted her head back and peered at him, anxiety clear in her expression. "But *what* just happened? Where's the big baddie? Did I miss its arrival?"

He lifted his shoulders in a shrug. "I don't know. Maybe it's a girl, and it changed its mind." Jenny stepped on his toes, and he grinned through his wince. "Or the doorway closed before it got through. I don't know. All I know is we're both still alive. And I, for one, am totally good with that."

"So what happens next?"

The whirling waves slowed their circular motion, and the circle of sand drew smaller and smaller, much like the hangman's noose, except instead of snapping their necks, they'd drown. Not a better alternative if you asked him. "I don't suppose you know how to fly?" he asked.

She shook her head.

"Got any scuba gear hiding around here?"

"Nope, and there's no way we can swim that far up before we both run out of air."

"I was afraid you'd say that. Then I guess we'd better pray."

"To who?"

"To me, I hope," boomed a voice.

What the hell was it lately with fucking people sneaking up on him! Felipe whirled to face the newcomer, some big, muscled surfer dude wearing a crown and sporting, of all things, a trident.

"Who the hell are you?" he snapped, not at all pleased at the tiny loincloth the tanned jerk wore.

"Most know me as Neptune, but Jenny can call me father."

Chapter Twenty-seven

In that moment, Jenny probably felt much like Luke did when Vader made his grand announcement. One big difference though? She didn't cry, "No!" On the contrary she seemed incapable of sound, although she tried. She opened and shut her mouth a few times at the announcement, much like a fish upon land. She probably should have said something, but who had time when the sea decided to take that moment to crash in on them? She had only a moment to grasp Felipe's hand when the cold water surrounded th—when warm air tickled them?

What in Neptune's—*daddy's ?*—beard was going on?

She and Felipe were encased in an air bubble while the sea swirled around them.

"Um, I take it you didn't do this?" he asked.

She shook her head. They both peered through the opaque side to see Neptune grinning at them and giving them a thumbs-up as he swam alongside their sphere. His legs had disappeared, morphed into a powerful fish tail, which propelled him upward, and despite not seeing any rope or anything attached to the bubble, he dragged them along with him.

The bubble burst from the waves and floated, up, up, then POP-ped! Jenny might have landed on her butt as she tumbled to the deck, but Felipe, who always landed on his feet, caught her.

"Okay, that was totally unexpected," Felipe said.

Understatement, which said a lot, given the events of the past week or so. "Where are we?" she asked, peeking around at the large boat deck, partially covered in goop and swarming with singing Vikings pushing large brooms. As someone screamed and fell from a mast, probably because both his hands clutched at his ears, Jenny winced and scrabbled for the amulet she'd stashed in her pocket. Miraculously enough, it had survived the turmoil. She slid it over her neck, lest she accidentally kill her allies.

A distinguished looking male, who might have appeared more impressive without the yellow slicker adorned with horned little duckies, approached them with arms wide and a big grin— which really didn't reassure. Jenny inched closer to Felipe.

"Welcome aboard the *S.S. SushiMaker*. So glad you both survived."

"Who is he?" she whispered.

It didn't take the flash of flames in his eyes or the melodramatic grab of his heart for Jenny to suddenly clue in. "Kill me now! Or not. It seems it's not just my daughter who needs the PR department to step up their game or face eternal torture. I am only the one and only, mighty Dark lord, king of the underworld, the punisher of sins, the—"

"Oh, can it," muttered a lovely woman dressed in a filmy green gown. "That's Lucifer, and I'm Mother Earth, but you may call me Gaia."

A familiar bikini-clad brunette held up a hand. "And I'm—"

"Lucifer's daughter. A pleasure to meet you!" Jenny said, unable to hide her delight.

"Hold on a second. You know Muriel but didn't recognize me?" Smoke curled from the devil's nostrils.

"Uh, well, yeah. My aunts and I have been following her exploits for years. She's quite the celebrity on the isle."

And as irreverent as the media claimed, or so Jenny judged when Muriel stuck her tongue out at Lucifer and said, "In your face. Finally someone who recognizes greatness."

"Anyone care to fill us in on what happened? I missed it when the flash of light closed the hole. Did we stop whatever was on the other side from coming through?" Felipe asked.

Judging by the exchanged glances and shrugs all around, no one quite knew. At least those on deck.

Neptune, who'd swapped tail for legs, approached their group on the ship's deck. "Seeing as how we're all accounted for and not under attack, I'd say whatever was attempting to come over failed."

Lucifer cleared his throat. "Yes, as my old salty friend here said, nothing happened. I, on the other hand, might cause some damage if I don't get some food. Anyone in the mood for sushi?"

Given the number of groans, not really.

"Something is rising on the starboard side," shouted the look out from his post.

What now?

Felipe's fingers curled around hers as they joined the others in leaning over the rail for a peek. From the roiling waves emerged a slick white sub.

"Who the fuck owns that?" Lucifer asked.

Jenny knew, and she couldn't help but smile as she yelled, "Hold your fire."

A good thing she'd remembered to put on her amulet, else she might have inadvertently killed a good portion of Lucifer's navy. As it was, many still winced, but at least no stray shots went flying and no more bodies dropped from the crow's nest.

"Do you know who that submarine belongs to?" asked the Lord of Hell with a frown.

A reply wasn't needed as the hatch flung open and from its depths emerged—

"Aunt Molpe, you are alive!" More moans accompanied Jenny's happy exclamation, but only one demon was overcome enough to fling himself over the side.

"Of course, she's alive," grumbled Thelxiope as she emerged just behind Molpe. "As if we'd let those water breathing sea-whores keep her. No one messes with my sister and lives."

As Jenny leaned over the rail to wave at her four aunts, overjoyed at their safety, she couldn't help but laugh as Lucifer grumbled. "No fair. They have a sub? How come I don't have a sub? How am I supposed to demand and inspire respect when you women have cooler toys than me? This is so unfair."

Neptune tossed an arm around his shoulder. "I agree, dude. But I have something they don't have. Mortal realm scotch from an English naval wreck. Care to share a glass while we discuss business affairs?"

"Shouldn't we talk about what tried to come through the rift and what we're going to do to make sure it doesn't try again?" asked Muriel, trailing behind them. "I've got a vacation to return to, and I'd like to know I can actually enjoy it without getting interrupted with a need to come to your rescue again."

"Rescue? Ha. The only thing that needs saving is me, from the machinations of your mother as she tries to drag me to the altar. I mean, who ever heard of such a thing, the devil getting married? Respectability," he shuddered, "is something no man should ever suffer."

As Lucifer strode off with Neptune, his tirade on the horrors of marriage loud enough for Gaia to hear, and smirk about, Muriel telling him to get his head out of his ass and focus on important matters, while Vikings cracked some barrels of ale and goblins swept the deck, Jenny leaned against Felipe. The one solid, real thing in a world gone mad. A crazy, messed up world that at the same time was wonderful because of the man who stood by her side. The man who'd come for her. The man who'd risked his life out of love and not because of a spell compelling him.

"What just happened?" she murmured.

"Welcome to just another day in Hell."

"You mean this type of thing happens all the time?"

"This exact scenario? No, but chaos, fighting, adventures, and Lucifer driving Gaia mental? Yes. Finding out your father is Neptune? I'll admit, that one was a surprise."

No kidding. She was still trying to wrap her head around that particular tidbit. A father? For so long she'd lived without one and given her mother's vitriol when asked, never gave it much thought. Now, to actually have a name and person to fill the role? She wasn't quite sure what to think or do about it. "Is he going to expect me to call him dad and return with him to the ocean do you think?" she asked, casting Felipe a worried glance.

"You're not going anywhere or doing anything you don't want to," he promised, his gaze solemn. "Unless you don't want to do me. Then, in that case, expect me to try and change your mind."

Her lips quirked. "And just how would you manage that?"

"How about by saying I was an idiot for thinking I could let you go. It turns out I don't want to be a roaming tom cat anymore. I want to be your pussy."

She laughed.

He made a face. "Okay, that did not come out right. I realized something when I thought I'd never see you again. I didn't like it. Somehow, during the course of our adventure, I fell in love with you." He peered anxiously at the sky.

"What are you looking for?"

"Don't laugh, but I often said, the day I declared my love for a woman was the day I'd get hit by lightning."

Jenny placed a hand on his heart. "You're still alive, and so am I, alive and in love with you."

"Really?"

She nodded her head. "And you don't have to give up roaming for me. Other women, yes," she corrected with a laugh. "But I wouldn't mind traveling by your side and seeing what Hell has to offer."

"Anyone ever tell you that you're perfect?"

"Only one man. The only one that counts. You."

"Finally, she listens."

"Don't expect me to make it a habit," she joked as she tilted her face for a kiss. Their lips touched, and there it was, the lightning he'd expected. It hit them both with a jolt, of arousal and need.

It didn't take the cheers from the Vikings watching to realize the passion between them needed a more private spot. Luckily for them, Lucifer, whom it seemed harbored a matchmaking fetish, had set aside a room for them. It wasn't discreet, not with the flashing neon sign he'd erected in the corridor they entered below decks saying, "Jenny and Felipe's Love Nest this way!" but it proved most definitely welcome.

They'd no sooner entered the small cabin than they fell on the bed, his heavier weight pinning her body to the mattress while his lips hungrily devoured hers. Hot breath mingled, tongues meshed, and their bodies molded, rubbed, frictioned, and delighted. How long they spent holding each other tight embracing she couldn't have said, but at one point, she couldn't ignore her body, which clamored for more. As if sensing her burgeoning need, Felipe slid his lips from her mouth and went exploring the column of her throat. Licks and nips, teasing caresses, a gentle bite of her racing pulse. Her breathing hitched.

"I'm going to make you sing," he growled as he shifted his weight to the side so he could tear at the remaining shreds of her toga.

"Promise?" was her wanton reply.

He chuckled against her lips as he crouched over her, the hair on his chest abrading her bare breasts. Her nipples were taut, protruding buds, begging for attention. And lavish them with his undivided attention he did, sucking at them. Drawing them into his mouth and swirling his tongue around them.

When he'd gotten his fill, and her writhing on the sheets, he moved lower, rubbing his face on the soft skin of her belly, a teasing pause to what she knew would come.

In an unexpected move, he rolled her onto her stomach and placed a kiss on each of her cheeks. He thrust an arm under her, hoisting her buttocks while keeping her upper torso flat on the bed. It surely exposed her to his view and just knowing he could stare at her sex, moistened it.

"You smell so sweet," he growled as he pressed his face against the crease of her thighs, his moist tongue tickling her skin. "Spread your legs," he demanded. A command she was more than happy to obey.

Even more exposed, she couldn't help but make a mewling sound as his warm breath fanned over her sex. But that was just the beginning. The wet tip of his tongue traced the outer edges of her sex. Teasing her. Arousing her.

When he finally did lick her—a wet, raspy swipe of his tongue against her sensitive flesh—she cried out. "Yes!" And more. She wanted more, but she didn't need to say it aloud. He knew. He acted. He pleasured.

Over and over, he lapped at her, his tongue probing between her lips, thrusting into her sex while Jenny clutched at the sheets, her body afire with desire.

His mouth latched onto her clit, and she bucked, but his greater strength held her in place, where he wanted her so he could suck on her sensitive flesh. She couldn't help it. A mini, shuddering orgasm went through her, a ripple of relief that did nothing to really sate her need. For that she'd need something inside her. Something only he could give her.

"Please, Felipe." She openly begged for it.

"So soon? Wouldn't you prefer to come on my tongue again?" he teased, his breath tickling her moist flesh as he slid two fingers into her welcoming channel.

"I'd rather come on you," was her honest reply.

She couldn't miss his tremble, not with their bodies touching in so many places. She tossed a looked over her shoulder and saw him staring at her, his eyes ablaze.

"Make love to me, Felipe," she murmured in a husky voice.

"I'm going to do more than that," was his guttural reply. "I'm going to mark and claim you so all of Hell, and anyone who sees you, knows you are *mine*."

Words shouldn't have the ability to trigger a second mini orgasm. His did. And she knew he felt it on his fingers by the way his lips curved into a self-satisfied smile. He pulled his fingers from her sex and licked them, a cat enjoying some cream.

Impatient, she waggled her bottom and shimmied back so that his jutting cock brushed against her. She wiggled some more, and he caught the hint. The head of his shaft prodded the entrance to her sex. He seemed determined to take it slow.

But she was so close to her third edge. She needed him inside. "If you don't fuck me," she muttered crudely, "I'm going to finish without you."

"Like fuck." He sheathed himself in one fell swoop.

By all the shells in the sea, it felt good. She couldn't help but gasp at the sensation. He filled her so snugly and deeply. He'd buried his cock to the hilt, and her channel clenched around him, ecstatic that it had something to cling on to. He dug his fingers into her hips as her pussy squeezed him. However, tight fit or not, it didn't stop him from moving. In and out he thrust, sheathing and withdrawing his hard length, each slap against her buttocks drawing forth a moan from her. As he increased his pace, Jenny's breathing came faster and faster. Her fingers dug at the sheets looking for purchase, her breasts swayed as he hammered into her welcoming flesh, the pressure built within her. Built and ... exploded.

Jenny tried to scream into the mattress. It muffled some of the sound, but when Felipe drew her up and curved himself to her back so he could bite her neck as he came, that scream, amulet or not, emerged with a decibel level to break windows.

And pierce a few eardrums of the demons nearby.

But, lost in the pleasure of their joining, cuddled, and in love, neither gave a damn. Hell's kitty had claimed his mate, and Jenny, for one, wouldn't hide who she was, not anymore.

Because I've finally found someone who loves me as I am.

Epilogue

The *S.S. SushiMaker* limped into the dock, and Lucifer tried not to grumble too much about the damage, especially once Neptune said he'd pay for it. Only right considering his daughter and her new lover caused most of it.

But the broken vessel, loss of hearing in a few dozen minions, and the babbling of a few dozen others was worth it. He'd paired his rascally Hellcat with Neptune's daughter. A daughter who would soon learn her mommy wasn't whom she thought.

Damn that girl possessed a fine set of lungs, lungs they'd still have a use for, or so his seers claimed. It was why he had Felipe fetch her in the first place. Of course, he didn't tell her that. Instead, when Jenny asked him what task he had for her, he'd told her she was required to teach the damned lovebirds Gaia insisted upon having in a cage in their bedroom, to sing. Cute and chirpy did not make for boudoir music. He hoped some of Jenny's warped ability would rub off on them.

A lie she actually believed. *Which is why I'm the king of fibs!*

The camera crews were waiting for him as Lucifer descended on a cushion of air, his rakish cape—which he'd swapped his ducky slicker for—fluttering in the breeze off the Styx. Microphones were thrust into his face. Flashbulbs went off, and he smiled, wide and frighteningly, to the delight of the rapacious reporters.

"Dark Lord, what can you tell us about the mighty battle?"

"Did you cause mayhem and carnage?"

He struck a majestic pose, arched a brow, and in a sarcastic tone he should have copyrighted before Hollywood stole it said, "We won, of course."

More or less. But Lucifer didn't elaborate, simply strode for his castle, his lady on his arm. Gaia smiled and waved at the crowd—she did so enjoy the spotlight much as she denied it. She kept him upright when a particularly brave reporter—who would regret her question later—yelled, "Rumor has it Mother Earth has been wedding dress shopping. Does this mean you've set a date?"

Before he could ask Gaia what the Hell, she waved her hand and transported him to their bedroom, the only one with the power and permission to do so in the first ring. She used it to her advantage, distracting Lucifer with a coy striptease before she wandered into his bathroom naked. However, he didn't join her, not with everything on his mind.

Yes, he'd succeeded in pairing yet another minion in the hopes of powerful babies, and yes, he'd saved the day, even if he didn't win the submarine in that game of poker with those Sirens. He knew they cheated. They had to have to beat him. If he weren't torturing himself with commitment, he might have shown them how much he liked their bending of the rules.

Yet, even losing wasn't what had him troubled. Ever get the nagging sense you'd missed out on a clue? A key element that would have made everything clear? He did, but for the life of him couldn't figure it out.

"I'll let you have some of my pie for your thoughts," Gaia murmured, strolling past him clad in only a towel.

"When did you have time to cook?" he asked, sniffing the air to see what kind she'd made.

"And to think you're an almighty ruler," muttered Gaia. "I didn't mean a pastry pie. I meant the other kind."

"Oh. *Oh.*" A leer stretched his lips.

"Those must be serious thoughts if your mind actually managed to stay out of the gutter for once. I'm assuming this has to do with the talk you and Neptune had over that bottle of booze."

"More like case of booze. That man has access to the most amazingly aged stuff, you know."

"And you haven't answered my question. What came through the rift?"

"Nothing."

"Are you seriously lying to me?"

"I'm the devil. Since when do I tell the truth?"

She glared at him.

"Fine, something came through to this plane all right. I just don't know what or where it went. As far as I can tell, which isn't much, some kind of presence did make it in before the rift shut. Whether or not it was the entity we feared though is unknown."

"And you have no idea where it went?"

He shrugged. "How the fuck would I know? It was the equivalent of a ghost and a tiny speck of one at that. It could have taken up residence in a crab for all I know."

Gaia wrapped her arms around Lucifer from behind, a subtle reminder of her support. A support he'd never admit aloud he might need. He created the man card rules, and they clearly stated that anything with a dick should stand on his own two feet. But there were times when being flat on his back with a luscious vixen in control atop him was fine too.

Oh and what did that have to do with the thing that worried him? Nothing, but it was a nice distraction.

"You're worried."

"Me? Nah. I thrive on the unknown. Live for danger. Come alive in battle."

"As well as worry about those you care about getting caught up in the power-hungry struggle of yet another entity looking to usurp your spot."

"Damned upstarts. I created Hell. Made it what it is today. They think they can just come along and fucking take what's mine."

"Like Hell."

"Fucking A, like Hell! I just wish the bloody bastard had the balls to show himself."

"Or herself."

"Whatever. All these omens and games and hiding behind minions. What's wrong with a good old-fashioned, one-on-one battle?"

Gaia circled around to stand in front of him and arched a brow. "A battle between two all-powerful deities? You know as well as I the repercussions of such a fight would have a ripple effect not just on the Hellish plane, but all the planes connected to it."

"It's been awhile since the Earth's had a good shaking. Which reminds me, don't we have dinner plans?" He leered at her.

She slapped his roaming hand aside. "My pie isn't ready yet."

It would only take a few kisses to rectify that. "But I'm hungry. And you said I could have some."

"You will, when we're done talking. Besides, the longer you wait, the more you'll appreciate it." Gaia trailed a finger down his chest, and he simmered with lusty heat. "What are we going to do about this new menace?"

"We?"

"Yes, we. We're a duo. An unstoppable force. If you fight, then so do I."

It was times like these, when her eyes shone with battle lust, that he could almost use the L word. Then he got a grip and gave himself a mental slap.

"It's time to muster the legion."

"And how many minions does it comprise? Have your numbers rebuilt enough since the Lilith incident?"

"I don't know." An admission that galled him. "My standing army is still short. However, I know there are demons I can call in from the wilds. Once I find them. That's where Charon's son is going to come in handy."

"Adexios? That fool?"

"A fool who likes to count things according to his father. I'm going to send the little geek out in the field to tag and count all the able-bodied minions he can find."

"He'll never survive out there."

"Which is why I'm going to pair him with the biggest bitch I know."

Gaia slapped his arm. "Is that any way to talk to your girlfriend?"

"Not you. I'm talking about one of those uppity Amazon bitches. It's time I called Thora, their leader, on the favor she owes me. If anyone's qualified to keep Adexios' nerdy ass out of trouble, then it's an Amazon warrior."

"Oh, you're not thinking what I think you're thinking, are you?"

"You naked with your legs around my neck and my lips on your clit?"

"Lucifer! I meant you're not thinking of matchmaking one of those Amazon ladies to that poor boy, are you?"

"Yes." He grinned. "Now admit it."

"Admit what?"

"You're thinking about my suggestion of your legs trying to choke me while I put my tongue to better use."

"Am not," she huffed, yet unable to stop the hardening of her nipples which protruded enticingly through the thin fabric of her gown.

Lucifer sniffed. "I think your pie is ready."

"Only if you can catch it." With a giggle, Gaia ran off, and Lucifer, ever the horny devil, gave chase.

But not before turning his head a full one hundred and eighty degrees to look you in the eye. Yes, you. Because he's got something to say. "I'll be back."

The End…? Not quite.

For more information or books, visit EveLanglais.com

34148507R00127

Made in the USA
Lexington, KY
24 July 2014